SEVEN POMEGRANATE SEEDS

JASMINE GARCIA

Seven Pomegranate Seeds
By Jasmine Garcia
Cover Design: Jasmine Garcia
Copyright © 2018 by Jasmine Garcia

All right reserved. Without limiting the rights under copyright reserved above, no part of this publication may be reproduced, stored in or introduced into a retrieval system or transmitted, in any form, or by any means (electronic, mechanical, photocopying, recording, or otherwise) without the prior written permission of the copyright owners of this book.

This is a work of fiction. Names, characters, places and incidents either are the product of the author's imagination or used fictitiously. Any resemblance to actual persons, living or dead, business establishments, events, or locales is entirely coincidental.

LICENSE NOTES

This book is licensed for your personal enjoyment only. This book may not be resold or given away to other people. If you would like to share this book with another person, please purchase an additional copy for each recipient. If you're reading this book and did not purchase it, or it was not purchased for your use only, please purchase your own copy. Thank you for respecting the author's work.

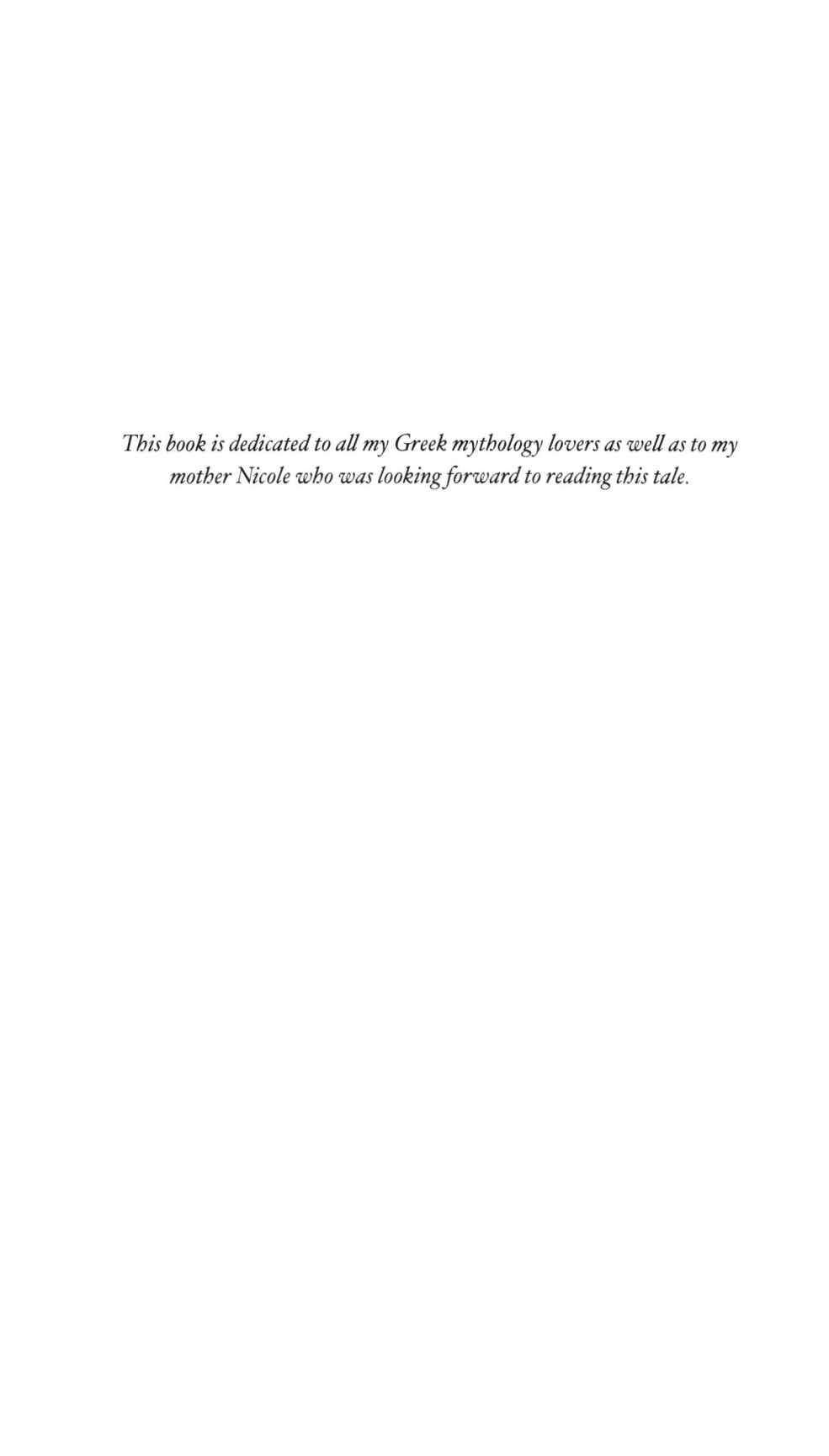

This book is dedicated to all my Greek mythology lovers as well as to my mother Nicole who was looking forward to reading this tale.

ACKNOWLEDGMENTS

Thank you to Alexandria, Cassidy, Samantha, Daniel, and all my other friends and family who have supported and encouraged me throughout the process of this book as well as my writing career in general.

Queen of the Underworld
Goddess of Spring
Flowers weaved in her veins
Pomegranate stained tongue
An ode to the undead King

Chapter One
AMONGST THE PEONIES

Amongst the peonies and lavender grass, where the blinding light of heaven bled down from Olympus, a young girl strayed aimlessly around the fields. Her bouncing, earthy-toned tresses followed her movements, tickling her rosy cheeks that matched the pink shade of her dress. She tilted her face up to the golden waves that rained over the psychedelic patterns of the many flowers, the warmth casting over her soft cheekbones.

At the tender age of fifteen, when her body was still shaping in her soon-to-be adorning curves, was when she first met him. She had strayed from her mother Demeter, plucking precious flowers from the ground to weave into the crown she wore. She placed them gently into the basket she held, continuing to stray towards the edge of the field. It was nearest to the end of the pasture that a menacing fault hidden in the tall wheat caught her curious eye, her smile reflecting the beam of the sun.

It was questionable to be so near a deep slit in the earth, but still, she rested on her stomach, gazing into its darkness. She felt not unsafe or weary but drawn to the abyss.

She stared into its blackness for a moment, admiring how it

contrasted to the brightness of the meadow when two vivid azure irises brought her to gasp in surprise. They, however, did not chase her off like they would have done many others.

Instead, she reached into her basket, drew the prettiest indigo peony from the posies, and inclined forward towards the stranger with the malevolent eyes.

A black hand that blended into light-colored skin manifested from the shadows, his long charcoal claws stretching to gently clinch the stem of the flower she was giving him.

Persephone giggled, and it was then she saw his eyes light up like the surrounding flowers.

"Persephone!" Persephone snapped her gaze over her shoulder to find her scowling mother advancing towards her. "What did I tell you about wandering off, girl?!" Persephone averted her cinnamon-colored orbs back to the fault. The pair of eyes suddenly reverted to their foul and lifeless appeal before they faded back into the blackness of the ground.

Persephone frowned, peering around to see if she could see the being one last time, but they had fled.

Her mother gripped her shoulder and drew her back, her worry filled expression morphed with rage. It was something Persephone was used to since she never abided by her mother's wishes.

"One day, someone will snatch you up, Persephone. Is that what you want?" Persephone smiled at her mother, completely disregarding her warning.

"Mother, I saw someone! They were right down the-" Persephone had returned her gaze to the crack that was no longer there, rather it was just smooth and unblemished ground. The abyss had completely vanished!

"Oh, Persephone. How your head is always in the clouds." Her mother scolded, hoisting her to her feet and dragging Persephone behind her. Persephone had clutched her basket, staring over her shoulder.

She knew what she had seen was not part of her imagination. And she was right to believe so.

The supposed figment was no other than Hades. God of the Underworld.

Chapter Two

HADES

"You asked me what I would like as a gift. I want to see what the world is like beyond this glass." Persephone pleaded, motioning to the lively town just outside their window. "Or at least allow me to explore this town on my own. I will be home before dark."

Demeter placed down the sewing needle she used to stitch a hole in one of her daughter's many gowns, and sternly glanced at Persephone. Her daughter fidgeted with the skirt of her dress, standing across the splintered table of their humble home. "I've told you many times, you cannot leave this house alone. You don't understand the dangers that are out there, Persephone." Demeter picked up the needle and resumed her work. "You're too beautiful to let this world taint you."

Anger clenched the maiden's fists, the anxious wringing of her dress halting.

"Mother, at least allow me outdoors. I am a young woman now." Persephone tried to reason, for tomorrow was the day of her twenty-second birthday.

"That is why you cannot leave all alone. Mortals are greedy, they will defile you." Persephone crossed over to her mother's side, hovering over her.

"I won't go far, mother. I will stay close by-"

"The answer is no, Persephone."

Persephone's eyes pricked with tears. In all her years she has never asked for anything. She was never one for gifts, and the one time she desired a single wish, she was turned away.

"How will I find a suitable candidate to wed if I don't visit elsewhere?" Demeter raised a brow, looking to her daughter.

"Silly girl, you are not marrying a mortal. You will marry into Olympus when I decide it will be fit." Persephone's heart sank at her words. She held no interest in any of her family on Olympus, she barely knew any of them. How could her mother do such a thing? Demeter would surely choose who took her daughter's heart, and Persephone would have no say. That, or she would never be married. That is how it always had been with her mother.

"I don't need you holding my hand! I can think for myself. I can determine what is right and wrong for me."

Her mother continued mindlessly sewing.

"You are still naive, dear child. Please, now fetch me more thread-"

Persephone stood back from her mother, clear streaks staining her blushed cheeks.

"No. I will not be forced into a loveless marriage. I will not end up like you, loving a man who doesn't love me!"

Demeter shot up from her chair and struck Persephone, the force of her harsh hand turning Persephone's face off to the side. A faint pink handprint stung Persephone's face, unshed tears wavering in her wide eyes. The wobbly chair in which her mother sat rocked to and fro, its creaking filling the tense silence between them. Persephone glared at her mother, Demeter's face scrunched in ire.

Demeter then silently returned to her seat, resuming her task.

"Go to your quarters. I don't wish to see you for the remainder of the night."

Persephone hitched up her gown and stormed off. Her mother's words would be the same ones that permitted Persephone to leave.

She would not see Persephone for most of her twenty-second birthday.

A garden had grown in the patch of sunlight that seeped in from the light above, dwelling into his personal Underworld. It plagued the filthy stone with beauty, disguising the rust stains of his victims with crimson roses that held the sharpest thorns. Grass pushed from beneath the flooring, uprooting the rocks to sprout daffodils, dandelions, and wildflowers that were a sore to his eyes. He despised the presence of it, but he never dared to step into the warmth of the light again.

Hades looked down at the indigo peony that had lived for the seven years in which he had held it, allowing the kind gesture to reside deep in the pocket of his cloak. He could still feel the affable touch when her fingers grazed his own. How it enlivened his dead heart with rapturous beats.

The memory nauseated him.

He has not dared peer into the bright light from then on, avoiding it at all costs, as if he would burn if he got too close.

"My Lord." Hades flickered his dark blue gaze towards an oaf by the name of Demokritos, a horned demon who managed the passageway between the mortal world and the Underworld.

"What is it, Demokritos?" His white eyes ringed with clear irises were wide in the direction of Hades, his blue lips stuttering before he managed to get his words out.

"There's a young goddess who is dying of asphyxiation, should I send her back to the mortal world?" Hades scoffed, his entertained expression never wavering.

"Since when did I ever care for those of Olympus? Might as well just give her a plot amongst the other souls early."

Demokritos' hoofs tapped as he turned, obeying Hades orders. As the clunking echo softened, in his peripheral, he noticed the space where the sun beamed was growing oddly dim, Hades' smugness mirroring the gradual fading of the godly light. It couldn't have been becoming night, for if it were, even the moonlight would be cascading over the flowers in a cool brightness. And then he noticed the flowers. Their dying petals wilted, fluttering into the drying grass that was becoming brown.

Hades reached into his pocket and found the plucked peony that had lived for seven years without nourishment, was crumbling in his hand.

His Underworld was becoming blackened by the second, the dead pieces of peony flying from his hand as he ran for the hall lit by blue flamed torches. He dashed fast enough to have his sapphire jeweled crown made of skulls fall and clatter against the stone ground.

His cape whipped against the wind until he arrived at Demokritos' side. Hades roughly shoved him aside just as his claws pushed through the soul barrier to grab the translucent wrist of the once young girl, now a beautiful woman with curves filling her form. He recognized her tight coils of curls, her full hair flowing around her, and shielding parts of her face. The blue hue in which souls manifested themselves here in the Underworld, snatched the soft shade of tan from her skin that had been exposed to the sun. She was gurgling, clutching her throat, and then he knew. She was drowning. Their eyes locked and though she was looking right through him, Hades felt as if she could see him and without a moment's hesitation, he stepped into the pathway that guided dead souls here, while Demokritos clutched his sleeve harshly.

"My Lord, you should not be seen in the mortal world. You understand that Zeus will smite you considering that is his daughter." Hades' eyes lit up, and suddenly this was no longer about saving the young woman. His viper eyes became slits and a grin lit up his eyes.

"Zeus' child. That is her?"

"Yes, daughter of Demeter and Ze us." Hades allowed his forked tongue to lick his lips.

"All the more reason to go and taste the lovely fruit, hmm?" Hades had never been close to his family. Cronus wasn't the best of fathers, considering he devoured Hades, and all of his siblings aside from Zeus. Zeus had been lucky enough to avoid the glutton, their mother Rhea replacing Zeus with a rock to ensure he lived far from the mouth of Cronus. After Zeus returned from hiding, he fed his father poison, causing Cronus to spit up his children. The only bond that he and his brothers shared was their hatred for Cronus. Soon after overthrowing their father and slaying him, that bond was broken, Zeus and Poseidon having cheated him. Each had drawn straws to gain ruling over Olympus, the sea, and the Underworld, Hades convinced he was set to earn the shortest of them. Hades had then turned his ire towards Zeus, and he most certainly despised Poseidon. All of Olympus had become sickening to him since he had been cast out. That, however, would be a story for another time.

Right now, he noticed his conquest's lips were growing blue under the strain of not breathing.

Hades dusted Demokritos' hand away and slipped into the path of pleading souls, making his way to the human world.

If there's anything that would please him more, it would be to toy with the daughter of Zeus just to crawl under his skin. Both he and Hades' twin sister, Demeter, were targets of his unhappiness, and he wanted them to feel what he's felt for hundreds of years.

Pain and anguish.

Hades reached the end of the path and was thrown into the mortal world, a black fog washing through the air.

He looked up at the blackness shielding the heavenly light that once blighted the sky, bringing him to cast his cold gaze towards a lake. Ripples were breaking the calmness in the center, weak splashing catching his eyes. The flowers surrounding the lakes edges were dead, dried up and withered like prunes.

Hades snickered, removing his cloak and dropping it aside before he rolled up the sleeves of his black shirt to his elbows. Hades stepped towards the quivering lake, diving in. The water was frigid, but it bothered him none since he was rather used to abnormal temperatures in the pits of the Underworld. His blue flames resided to his core, shriveling up against the water currents as his serpent eyes scanned the murky waters. It was when a white cloth caught his eyes that he pushed himself to swim towards it. Upon growing closer, he noticed her dark locks and subtly tanned skin.

It was her.

Hades saw the light disappearing from her eyes, swiftly gripping her waist and drawing her close so he could swim her back to shore.

He swam to the surface, taking in a sharp breath before he turned to the unconscious girl, swiping her wet tresses from her graying face.

Hades pushed himself towards the grassy ledge, drawing her out of the water first, laying her limp body on the grass before he climbed out after her.

He stared at her lifeless body, scratching his drenched hair in confusion.

He's taken many lives, but saved one? Never had he done so.

Cautiously, he knelt at her side and rolled her onto her stomach. Harshly he struck her back.

He expected he retrieved her too late when she didn't respond to the firm blows he delivered in order for her to spew the water from her lungs. With one final blow, she winced and sputtered a frothy mixture of saliva and water. She coughed and gasped, her wheezing lungs burning from being subjected to the tortuous task of drowning.

Hades was relieved, but all the wrong words came from his mouth.

"You're an imbecile." Her dreary cinnamon gaze met with his, her face not hesitating to scowl. Quickly her expression became one of awe.

"Hades." Hades rolled his azure orbs, one's in which she would never forget. "If you could not swim, what would possess you to dive into the middle of the lake. Were you that desperate for a death sentence?" His hardened expression brought her to cough and sit up from her position in the muddied grass. Gradually, the browning blades were beginning to become green with life yet again.

She wordlessly reached into her dress and plucked out a copper coin. Immediately he knew what it was.

A token for the town's seers.

"You asked why I would endanger my life?" A grin curled her plump lips. "Well, you're here now, aren't you, Lord Hades? Do you have time for a quick tale?"

Persephone laid awake in her bed, night after night playing the same event for the past seven years. Ever since she had encountered him, her mind never ventured anywhere else. She just wanted to know who he was, and the question ate at her day after day because no matter who she asked, everyone just deemed her to be silly and imaginative. Her mother and father included. Zeus and Demeter told her to keep her imagination on a leash and focus on the bright future ahead she would have on Olympus.

She's even tried to research what tricks her mind may have caused her in various books, but there was nothing of him.

Eventually, she was starting to believe she did just concoct the entire event.

That was until the day of her twenty-second birthday.

Persephone tossed and turned in her sleep after the ugly argument with her mother, before she woke abruptly. She would be expected to wed soon, and she couldn't just let go of the possibility that there was someone she had met before.

That night, she flew out of bed, tiptoeing passed the room of her sleeping mother to tear her cloak from the back of a dining room chair, heading into the chilly night.

She spotted her local merchant beginning to pack up her stall amidst the empty streets, and Persephone flew towards her, assuring the hood of her brown cloak hid her face.

"I apologize for the late request, but I was curious as to if you would have a token of the seers." The woman paused, a wide smile revealing a mouth full of missing teeth, the few she did have lined in gold.

"For the right price, I may have one." Her raspy tone teased, to which Persephone sighed, reaching into the satchel she had strung around her.

She felt a few pieces of cold metal graze her fingers, and she snatched them into her hand, holding out three silver coins to the merchant.

"This is all I have." She pleaded. Persephone needed to hurry before her mother woke, or before the seers refused to see another customer for the night, neither of which would be an outcome she favored.

The scraggly woman with thin graying hair lifted a crooked finger, pointing to the silver locket that peered from beneath Persephone's cloak.

"I believe that will cover it." Persephone instinctively reached up to hold the locket she had worn since infancy. It was a necklace to shield her from evil and ward off wicked beings whose intentions were foul.

What was more important to her? Being guarded, or fulfilling an inquiry she has desired to know for seven years?

Persephone ripped off the necklace blessed by her father and other gods before holding it out to the merchant.

In the end, temptation won. She was old enough to guard herself, she didn't need some silly necklace.

She would simply explain she lost it if anyone were to ask.

As promised, the merchant drew a copper token from her box, giving it to Persephone.

"Enjoy dearie. May the seers give you good fortune." And with that, they parted ways, Persephone taking off under the bright moonlight that *illuminated the sandstone path. It led her to the darkness of the forest, where the seers of Past, Present, and Future resided.*

Persephone took a deep breath, remembering the caution of being within this forest.

Some say locals went in and never returned, forever stuck in time within the forest. Those people would slowly lose their sanity and become one with the gangly trees to snatch in victims.

Persephone reached up for her necklace, however, it was no longer there to be her security when she needed it.

Creasing her brows, she puffed her chest and stepped daringly into the forbidden forest.

She didn't need a necklace to protect her. She could care for herself. The voice in her head reminded her. Nothing was going to stop her from getting her answers tonight.

One step after another, Persephone was making her way towards the eerie wooden house, balancing near the edge of the cliff where it was closest towards the moon.

The path was easy enough to follow; though she did get startling feelings of eyes watching her and claws grazing her back, she didn't let it unsettle her too much. She walked with her head held high. Evil sensed fear, and she wouldn't allow it to catch a whiff of hers.

Persephone strode at an easy pace, the pace to which her heart beat while her feet would occasionally sink into the mud.

Eventually, she did catch vision of the brittle wooden house through the fog that had begun to blur her vision.

She dashed then, not because she was afraid of what lurked behind her, but because she was so eager for answers.

Persephone journeyed through the woods not many have returned from and approached the house. She gave a series of raps on the door decorated with animal skulls and lavender grass.

The door was opened, and she was greeted by a woman with hair the color of the fiercest of flames, skin a ghostly wan, and eyes that resembled two deep jade stones.

"Persephone." She greeted warmly, though Persephone had never met

this woman in her life. Upon seeing her befuddled expression, the woman rested a friendly hand on her shoulder. "Future has told me about your arrival. You desire to know something regarding your adolescent years, yes? Come right in and Past will be able to give you some answers." Persephone handed the seer her token, following the woman into the cozy interior of the home.

Though the outside was thoroughly rough, the inside was warm and welcoming, a fire was set in the hearth and there was a table in the center of the home, a crystal ball inhabiting the table with four seats.

A woman with sleek midnight hair and the darkest of ebony skin sat in one chair, her right eye gone from her skull leaving a void hole to pair nicely with the black eye that existed on her left. Another woman sat beside her, one with fair skin, champagne locks, and a single golden eye, her left eye missing from her socket.

"The dark one is Past, and she is missing an eye because she cannot see the future, but she can see the past. The fair one is missing an eye because she cannot see the past but can see into the future." Persephone presumed the woman with beautiful orange hair at her side was Present. She took a breath to ask her a question when she was interrupted with an answer. "I have both my eyes because I can both see some of the past and predict some of the future since I am after all the present. I can give estimated outcomes." She brought Persephone to the table to sit, the goddess greeting everyone respectfully.

"Thank you for making time for me at this hour. I need to know the answer for it stirs me in my sleep and won't let me rest." Past lifted a hand and took Persephone's in her own.

"You desire to know about the creature you have seen within the fault of the ground when you were fifteen years of age, yes?" Her deep tone stunned Persephone, for these people could read her like a storybook, and she needn't say a word.

"Yes. He was real?"

"Very." Present replied. "You are playing with the flames of Hell dear girl. Best you steer away."

Persephone shook her head, past clutching her hand tightly before

Persephone could speak. She was staring off, not looking directly at Persephone as if she were stuck in another world.

"No. He holds kindness in his heart? Is that possible?"

"Who?" Persephone questioned anxiously.

"Him? Hold kindness in his dead heart? Ha!" Present snickered, however, Past was grim.

"Who?!" She said in a more demanding tone, her fist hitting the table and shaking the crystal ball. She had come here for answers and desired to have them.

"Hades." A gentler tone smiled. It was Future. "God of the Underworld." Her voice was so soft it soothed Persephone's wired nerves despite the information she was given.

"Hades?" Hades was an abomination. At least that is what her father had said. No one spoke of him. No one even uttered his name for he was such a disgrace. That is all she knew. His name. There were no tales told of him. No myths. Nothing. It was as if he did not exist. She had searched when she had heard his name spoken by another God but gave up the search quickly. "Why can't I find tales of him anywhere? It is almost like he is erased from this world altogether."

"Try asking another question. That is not our story to tell. An inquiry about the past, present, or future will do." Persephone pursed her lips.

"Will I meet him again?" Future tilted her head to the side, adapting the glazed look in her eyes.

"Unfortunately, yes. You seek him, and so he will come. Place your life in danger, and he shall follow willingly, crawling from the depths of Hell to obtain his conquest." Future brought her eye back to Persephone. "That is all I know. The rest is unclear."

Present and Past also agreed that there was nothing left to say.

"We hope we have been of use to you." The three of them simultaneously uttered.

Persephone didn't even have time to perceive the information she was just given before she was thrown into a haze of blackness.

Persephone sat up in her bed, sweat soaking the sheets and dampening her dark locks. Her breathing was heavy, and when she reached up to touch her necklace, it was gone, and instead on her chest was a burned token, unusable for a second time.

As Persephone tried to catch her breath, she smiled, the sun shining brightly through her curtains to mimic her happiness. She held the token tightly in her hand, kicking away the covers. Future's words played freshly in her head over and over again as Persephone fled the house in her nightdress and out into the fields nearby.

"You seek him, and so he will come. Place your life in danger, and he shall follow willingly, crawling from the depths of Hell to obtain his conquest."

꙳

Hades had expected to be speaking with the same sweetened little girl he had encountered seven years ago, but the soaked maiden sitting before him wore a wicked expression.

"You're a fool. I should have allowed you to die, just so you could spend your eternity with me in the Underworld since that is what you appear to want." Hades growled, clutching her face in his palm. Persephone held his heated gaze and smiled.

"The thought excites me." Hades was stunned because many would be afraid and steer clear of him, but here she was, summoning him from the Underworld just to see him.

Hades let her face loose and slumped beside her, just for a short moment. "What is your name?"

"Persephone. Daughter of Zeus and Demeter." Hades visibly tensed at the name of his siblings with pure disgust.

"Loathsome beings they are." He grunted under his breath.

"Excuse me?"

"Persephone is your name?" He ignored her offended tone, Persephone huffing and nodding her head.

"Indeed."

"Is this all you wanted, Persephone? To see if I exist and fulfill your curiosity? Because congratulations to you, I exist, and you've done something so petty to tear me from my work." Persephone blinked her wet lashes, her beam unaltered.

"I knew you existed, Lord Hades. I just desired to see you once more in person. You're a rather intriguing character, I simply could not stop thinking about how you would appear to me, but I will say it was well worth the wait." She giggled. Hades ran his fingers through his flame riddled hair in annoyance, the blue licks of fire drying his drenched locks. He didn't have time for her little girl antics.

"I hope you're satisfied now, for I have no desire to come back to such a pitiful place." Persephone plucked a flower from the grass and held it out to him, this time the flower a white daisy.

"Please do come back. I truly would adore seeing you again." Hades was growing uncomfortable, and while he would blame it on the heat of the sun or the wetness of his clothes, the soft hue of pink in his death-colored skin gave away his true source of discomfort. He hadn't had anyone wish to visit them for if he did, it usually was because they were succumbing to death. "You make for entertaining company, Lord Hades. I hope that I have at least pleased you with my own. Even if it did inconvenience you." It was hard to tear away from the sincerity her eyes held. Nonetheless, he did, clutching his cloak from the ground.

Hades waved his hand to open the pathway to the Underworld, shaking his head.

"Goodbye, Persephone." He grumbled.

"I hope to see you soon, Lord Hades."

As he disappeared into the portal and walked past the crying souls that surrounded him, he could not waver his thoughts from the beautiful woman in which desired his company terribly enough to risk her life.

His thoughts were so jumbled, that his original plan to drag her to the Underworld to anger Zeus, had completely left his thoughts. That made him rather irritated.

He clutched his fists, preparing to turn around and snatch

her up, however, he continued down the dark path to the Underworld.

Her time would come, and when it did, he would have her then.

Hades snaked his tongue over his grinning mouth.

All to himself.

Chapter Three
SERPENTS & FLOWERS

It's been a month since he's seen Persephone, and each of those days he would find himself returning to the garden to check on the little patch of life, flowers returning to their full bloom and lively color.

It was small at first, but as each day passed, he noticed the flowers began to droop, the vivid hues becoming dull.

Today, the sun had darkened drastically.

He knew she wasn't trying to commit to another suicide attempt, for the flowers were still clinging to their roots, moist and watered. They almost appeared saddened.

Hades gave a heavy exhale that washed through the silent domain.

"Demokritos. Fetch me my cloak." Demokritos gave Hades a questioning quirk of his brow.

"You're not returning to the surface, are you?" Hades slicked his fingers through the blue flames engulfing his locks that resembled burned ashes, angered by Demokritos probing.

"It is none of your business what I do in my spare time, miscreant. Now hand it to me." He held his hand out to the demon.

Demokritos clunked over to him in a hesitant manner, which only pressed the annoyance Hades felt.

Flames roared over his entirety as he snatched his cloak from the shaking grip of the creature.

"Now go before I toss your flesh to Cerberus. Surely they would be hungry for a goat." Hades teased, biting his teeth at Demokritos as a dog would.

Hades decided he would not take the passage, for his presence would slow the souls from getting to their destination here in the Underworld. Rather, he would just have his chariot drag him to the top, and he would climb to the ledge.

With a snap of his fingers, his chariot was at his whim. Horses that were ghostly shadows with piercing midnight orbs neighed in protest. Flecks of ash scattered around them, formed from the fires, and darkness of the Underworld's flames. The chariot was as black as the horses, meant to blend in with the darkness he was so familiar with.

He climbed in, Demokritos still unsure of his antics as he closed the door behind him. His horses then shot up, galloping on the side of the walls that led to the surface.

Just as quickly as they traveled through the dark, they skidded to a halt at the presence of a dim light, to which Hades knew was all they would go. Though his horses could travel in the gloomy scenery, they preferred darkness, and he could not blame them.

He opened the chariot door and peered up, noticing the hike wouldn't be too long. They were close to the surface.

Huffing, he drew up the hood of his dark cloak lined with gold buttons and hiked up the side wall. He reached for the edge of the grassy plain, digging his fingers into the soft earth. It felt fleshy, an odd texture beneath his fingertips. He was so accustomed to rigid rock and bone, that it made a shiver race through him.

He only understood what death felt like. Life was something he had long forgotten about.

Putting his thoughts aside, he hauled himself up. He peered around, tilting his head, wondering why the sky was so gray when it was usually bright and yellow.

Nearby, he noticed a woman lying in the grass, fingers grazing the water as she sadly looked in at her rippling reflection.

From the tightly wound curls that sprawled along the dim grass, he already knew who it was.

"Persephone." The name had left his mouth so unexpectedly, it caused him to bite his tongue.

Persephone turned her solemn eyes from the water, to Hades who stood not too far away as he shielded the fault in the ground.

She sat up in excitement. Her eyes lit up and brightened the sun, the drooping flowers waking in their full bloom.

The light stretched over him, and though the warmth was odd and unfamiliar, there was something about it that gave him...comfort? What was this strange feeling? The flames of the Underworld did not give him the same feeling, and neither did the inner fire he bore.

The light then shined directly into his eyes, and he turned away rapidly with a hiss.

"Damn the Gods!" He sneered, wiping his watering eyes that were rather unadjusted to brightness.

"My apologies!" Persephone squealed, her tone mixed with both sympathy and elation. "I thought you would never come back." Hades unveiled his eyes to find Persephone padding over to him. "I'm happy you returned." Persephone was standing unbearably close, which was uncomfortable to him. And then she did something that made him flinch.

She raised her hand to his face, stroking back his hood. Her fingers glided through his hair, threading through the midnight locks. "I didn't hurt you, did I? It completely fled my mind that it was dark down there. Is that better?" Her voice was a practical purr in his ear, the golden rays shielding behind clouds.

Hades took her wrist in his hold, blue flames licking her skin.

SEVEN POMEGRANATE SEEDS

Persephone ripped her touch away abruptly, and Hades eased his tense muscles.

She glared at him, rubbing her burned flesh.

"Much better." He confirmed, a smirk curling the corners of his lips.

"So why did you return?" She gritted painfully through her teeth.

Hades eyes scoped the surroundings of floral arrays and long wheatgrass.

"It would have appeared to me that you were sulking." He spat before he could even stop himself. This brought a smile to Persephone's full lips, her eyes glittering like sunlight against the reflective surface of water. "And having no sun would be awful for crop growth, wouldn't it? Hell is full enough, we don't need famine to drag in any more souls. I have enough to tend to." He quickly added in a poor attempt to cover up his prior reasoning.

"Oh, is that so? A month of dwindling sunlight would harm no crops, I assure you, Lord Hades. My mother would be sure crops thrived." She smiled playfully, and Hades' cast his eyes away. With blood rushing to his cheeks, he turned around and readied to take a trip back into the Underworld. He wasn't sure what else to say having been thoroughly humiliated by Persephone's teasing. "Please stay awhile, Lord Hades. I was just jesting." Persephone giggled, taking his hand, but quickly she snatched away remembering he wouldn't hesitate to burn her.

Hades looked down at the hand she touched, then back at her, holding her firm gaze, and wiped her touch on his black pants.

"For someone who desires my company surely is doing a great deal to chase me off." He snapped, irritated by her constant fiddling with him.

Persephone scoffed. "You act as if you've never had a lady touch you, but I am certain a man of your appearance and one who deals with sinners surely had his share of more than just hand-holding." Hades locked his jaw at her response.

"The women who I've encountered are not sweet fruits." Hades closed the distance between them now, it was her turn to feel discomfort. "I prefer my women to be filthy. As disgusting as street gutters. Your warmth is nothing but a bitter taste in my mouth." Persephone was fuming now, a blaze ignited in her eyes as he tipped up her chin. "You'd do very little to fill my appetite."

Persephone snatched from his grasp and an ire filled grin lifted her lips. "I think you're afraid I'd be too filling for you. That's why you're afraid to take a bite."

Hades forced her back into a nearby tree, towering over her.

"Afraid? A snake like me could swallow you in one bite." Persephone raised a challenging brow at his slit eyes and forked tongue.

"Then why haven't you?"

"Snakes don't eat fruit." Hades calmed the flames beginning to chew his skin beneath his cloak. "They eat flesh that rots."

"I have plenty of flesh to offer." Persephone drawled, and she wasn't deceiving him. She did offer delectable curves in her figure. She had won, and they both knew that.

Hades exhaled in irritability, shutting his eyes, and backing from Persephone. Coming here was a mistake.

"I know not much of you, Persephone. Why so interested in a serpent?"

"I could ask the same to you, Hades." She slipped from his grasp and sauntered over to the lake. "If you desire to know more, I am an open book to you. I am curious to learn more of you as well." Persephone granted, patting the grass beside her.

Hades relented, deciding he would humor her.

He made his way over to her side, the two sitting under the dull afternoon sun.

Persephone's victorious smile gleamed, even against the dreary sky that lacked its heavenly glow.

It gave his heart an odd twitch as he settled into the flowers, and watched her lips move.

Her defiance and bravery hadn't warned him off at all.

It only piqued his intrigue, and gave him what he believed was rapture.

The maiden was a fruit he wanted to taste the moment they had encountered. Even if he denied that to her.

Persephone, however, did not make any feeble attempts to hide her desires, for she too desired a taste of the sourness the mysterious God had to offer.

Chapter Four
HER OFFERINGS

"And so came that day. Even his own sons turned against him, the greed for power overbearing the blood they shared. Even after I assisted in slaying Cronus, I resented Zeus and Poseidon just as much, if not more." Hades eyes widened, having realized he had spoken an awful lot to her, sharing things he hadn't in years. He cleared his throat, her expression showing no signs of pity or curiosity. She merely stared out to the sunset across the river.

"My father mistreated you, hadn't he?"

"He has. Just as cruel as his father. Cheated me once I've helped them in their feats to overthrow Cronus. They made me God of the Underworld. One of death, sorrow, and misery, while they bathed in the light of heaven. Bitter, I returned to Olympus, and made it known," Hades clenched his fist remembered the bloodshed of that horrid event. "I made it known, I was never to be crossed again." He cocked his head back to her. "The thought of your father to be such a scoundrel is not much of a surprise to you, is it?" Persephone hung her head.

"It shames me to be in relation to such a ghastly God." Her piercing gaze flickered back to him. "But I will not apologize on their behalf. I am not like them. I harbor no such intentions towards you. I only wished for a confidante." The two both shared an equal hatred for Zeus. She just didn't realize how much she despised her father until Hades discussed the following, Hades describing just how treacherous her father was.

"Enough about my woeful past, my dear." He jested, dramatically resting his hand over his face. "Tell me, what do you have to offer?"

Persephone was quiet. She had not much to say of herself.

"My life was one of peace. I never did have quarrels, for I mostly was raised around humans. It would be my future to be granted a place on Olympus once I was wed." Persephone looked away now, the smooth petals of a flower being caressed between her fingers. "Only I do not wish to be forced." She grumbled irritability. "I know naught of who is to bed me and whose children I will bear, but I strongly feel Hera will introduce me to Poseidon." Her lips curled as did her fists. "Wench he is. I do not wish to bear his children."

It was almost inaudible to him, hearing her speak ever so softly over the gentle wind of the evening. "That is not love." Persephone released a huffed breath, then chuckled.

"My life is a bore." Turning to Hades, her expression became one of a mischievous imp. "I seek thrill and excitement. I can never find that here."

"Is that why you summoned me here?" Persephone gasped, having not expected his perplexed reply.

"I suppose." She returned to her eased mannerism, the pink tint in her flesh cooling to its sun-kissed hue. "I merely desired to know who it was that tempted me so. My curiosity filled the void in my life that lacked the rhythm I craved." She beamed, Hades amused by her honest tale.

He leaned towards her, taking her chin between his thumb and forefinger.

"Be careful what you wish for, Persephone." The slits of his pupils reveled in her ethereal beauty, his serpent tongue flickering past his bladed fangs to taste the air.

To his shock, buried beneath the aroma of flowers that caressed her skin, the redolence of rebellion and burning fields soaked into the roots of those flowers. The same hands that would stroke the flowers beneath her gentle fingertips could burn if she truly desired it enough with the defiance seeded deep within her.

She didn't bear that same tenderness he knew of when he saw her in the fields at the ripe age of fifteen. She was far from it now.

She bore the scents of home.

It was not Persephone who was stunned by his advances, in fact, she was calm upon seeing his snake-like scales crawl along his neck to his jaw and morph into his flesh. His features expressed his astonishment, and so rapidly, he snatched his being from her, relaxing back to his human qualities.

"Well, I've enjoyed our little chat, but it's time I return." As he got to his feet, Persephone's eyes burned to him.

"You will come back, won't you?" Hades halted, raising his snake engraved trident, readying to pierce the ground to create a fault.

"If I have the time." He murmured over his shoulder before he rammed the metallic weapon into the soil, bringing it to tremor.

Persephone gave him a half smile, returning her gaze to the setting sun.

"I will be patiently awaiting your arrival then, Lord Hades."

And the two parted ways yet again.

Late in the night, when the moon was highest in the sky, Persephone was awake, reveling in the darkness of her room. She sat close to the altar she had created just for him upon learning Hades' altar was destroyed by Zeus for his *"crude"* misdeeds. She heard whispers in the street if she listened close enough. The death of crops and sudden demise of cattle were all caused by the appearances Hades had made on earth, his godly strengths wreaking havoc without even noticing. Or maybe he simply didn't care for the well-being of mortals. They spoke about being elated that he was banished to the Underworld, happy he receives no pity or endearing gifts of worshipers, for he is a serpent who brings nothing but misery. Even after learning this, Persephone was enraged they treated him as if he were diseased. He was a God that gave a home to the dead. He should be treated with far more respect than he was being given.

It was all because of the words that dripped from her father's lips, spewing lies when in fact it was he that caused Hades to become destructive. Cronus was the original source of his foul behavior, but her father buried the stake in his back. If he was raised with kindness, maybe he would have been less bitter.

Possibly not.

No one can ever be alright after what he had been forced to endure. He was cursed from the beginning. Maybe this had always been his fate.

She lit the last black candle she obtained from the town's witch. A single flame on either side of her makeshift altar; made of a flat stone she found near a river, one she had searched for hours for. She desired perfection and this is as close as she had gotten. She placed blue wildflowers and stems of lavender upon the slab. Then, she reached into her satchel, where she had managed to hide a field mouse. Surprisingly, it had not become unconscious being in the enclosed space for so long, still squirming and squeaking.

She took the little brown creature in one hand, holding it to the coldness of the stone. The other fished for the small blade she carried with her.

What she would do next was rather disheartening, having never harmed any living creature, but she would soon be over it.

It's a kind gesture to him. She reminded herself. Animals were sacrificed in the name of the gods often. Sheep, cows, lamb, chicken, pig. This would be no different.

It would be a sign of devotion, while simultaneously turning her cheek to a father she no longer admired for his lies.

"I send thee to the Underworld, my offering to Hades." She murmured, piercing the blade through the little mouse. A sharp squeal exhaled before its life was expelled in the color of red. Droplets of blood had splattered onto her cheek, leading her to drop the knife, and wipe her face.

Persephone then leaned forward and pressed her lips to the bloodied stone. "Best send that as well." She tittered, straightening from the altar, and puckering her pillowy lips to blow out the candles until the wicks dimmed in orange.

The following weeks, Persephone repeated the sacrifices, each one growing easier than the last, for she knew she was doing the right thing in honor of his existence.

She shut her cinnamon orbs, and all she envisioned were his viperous slits and scaly skin that had revealed itself in her presence.

It brought her to shiver in delight.

He deserved this as much as any other God or Goddess.

🐍

Upon his canopy bed, the deep sapphire curtains were drawn back to a young woman sprawled out on the silken bedding. Their bare cocoa flesh was partially covered by the sheets, their arm lying over their breasts. Their lengthy braids that were tightly woven into their skull descended fluidly over the softness of the bed, while their earthy orbs followed his movements.

"Hades, I desire your company. Do I not please you?" Their plush lips pouted, eyeing him as he stood near his altar that was coated in cobwebs. It was something that had not held charity for hundreds of years.

"Cerberus, in all the years I have owned you, never have I

been interested in bedding you. You merely are a pet to me." Anyone who saw Cerberus in their womanly form would be foaming from the mouth, but the thought of their other two personalities prevented him from being interested.

"A pet?! That is all I am to you?!"

Cerberus, a Hellhound of three heads embodied three different human personas, was a present from Hera. A consolation gift that failed to stop him from destroying Olympus. The three personas consisted of a beautiful female with a rather quick temper, a fuse shorter than his own. The next was a quieter male, his hair dark and unruly with obsidian irises to match. His skin was amber, similar to the tone Persephone bore. He was well-built, broad shoulders, and muscular attributes to match. While he was quite the gentleman, he had no issues chewing out the throats of his enemies. He merely preferred to remain hidden most times, keeping to himself unless in their demon form. The last was a mute young man, neutral in build with blond locks and eyes blue as the flames of his master. He said not much, but he held the strength of a thousand men. He was built for war.

All of them made up the demon Hades called Cerberus, and when in their beast form, their combined attributes made for a lethal weapon of destruction.

From time to time, Hades would be surprised with either of the two young men, or woman form wandering the Underworld. Never could they all be out and about at once for they all shared one body.

He was more often than not greeted with the maiden on his bedspread unfortunately.

Quite the talker she was. She talked enough for her two counterparts.

"Hush now, Cerberus. You needn't shout." Hades' half-heartedly reprimanded, hovering over the third little mouse that had been sacrificed to him paired with lavender and blue flowers.

He already knew who the culprit was.

Their naked character crawled from bed, and moved towards the altar, hugging Hades from behind to peer under his frame at his gift.

"Another? Hmm. It appears you have an admirer aside from me." They snickered, snatching the dead mouse and tilting back their head to drop it into their hungry mouth. They bit down, a growl rumbling through their chest as redness stained their canines. It spilled from their lips, dripping onto their supple skin, as they crunched the bones with ease. "Is it from that Persephone maiden you appear to enjoy so much? Her name leaves your lips in your sleep." Cerberus' teasing led Hades to roll his eyes.

"I'm certain it does not."

"No? Then how would I possibly know her name? I am naught but a hound. I do not wield psychic abilities." He would never raise his hands to his trusted guard of the gates, nonetheless, it was growing tempting to strangle his pet.

"Cerberus, if you wish nothing but to irk me, do leave." Hades turned his heel from the altar, his cape whipping behind him.

"Alright. I bid you goodnight and will go to sleep." Hades grunted, beginning to undress for bed.

They exhaled dramatically. "On that awfully cold stone drenched in plague and bone,"

Hades affirmed he had heard them with another guttural sound.

"I'm going now." They said solemnly.

"Are you?" Hades grumbled. There was silence until he huffed in aggravation. "Get in and stop your sulking." He tugged the sheets to allow her in, Cerberus zipping under the covers beside him in elation.

Hades pet their locks as she drifted off as opposed to watching the gates tonight.

It wasn't too busy, and no visitors were expected, so there was no need for Cerberus to be waiting there when they needed rest. His other horned inhabitants would keep watch for the evening.

As he laid there in silence, he couldn't help thinking of the charity left for him the prior days.

It was something that hadn't been done since he had been banished from Olympus.

The gifts were small, yet meaningful to him. They made him feel desired, and he wasn't sure exactly how to deal with the emotion, so he brushed it aside.

Persephone was an odd woman, but she deeply piqued his interest, and with her current offerings it only brought him to grow more enveloped in thoughts of her.

He reached under his pillow, and grasped the tail of a dead rat, something he's hidden from the glutton beside him.

He cast a stern glare at their sleeping form.

Hades didn't desire to eat it. He wanted to save it, but it would only continue to rot here. That's what flesh did here in the Underworld.

Taking the small creature, he dropped it onto his tongue, and swallowed it whole, having no need for chewing with his snake-like abilities.

It was the first time in forever something filled his stomach.

He longed for such a feeling, and he couldn't remember how precious it was to have an offering given.

Hades nestled comfortably under the silk, allowing his thoughts to drift back to that sweetened smell of burning grasses, and sultry intent. She smelled like the Underworld. Like she belonged here.

His eyes rolled back with bliss, his lips curving into a ghost of a smile.

What started off in an attempt to anger Zeus, became something Hades could not control. He knew naught of what he felt for Persephone, unfamiliar with the adorning emotions.

But there was one thing he was sure of.

He was certain he wanted to see her again.

Chapter Five
OLYMPUS

"Mother, I really have no desire to go." Persephone whined as they approached the gates of Olympus, climbing the marble stairs to the glowing pillars.

"No desire to see your father?" There was that, especially having become infatuated with Hades. Even though he hasn't visited her much, she sensed his presence around.

Dead cattle, dying crops, sick civilians.

He was there with her.

Hiding in the shadows when she snuck out and made her nightly trips into town. She would occasionally catch a glimpse of his searing blue eyes, leading her to turn away with a smirk.

She wasn't afraid to go outside anymore like she had been when she was younger. Her mother always warned her of ravenous men, however, Persephone didn't fear them any longer. Hades was watching, and she knew he wouldn't let anything happen to someone who worshiped him as much as she. She felt invincible whenever he was around, and she adored that feeling very much. She craved it.

Persephone's beam was soon wiped from her face when they approached the white and gold double doors.

Not only did she have no yearning to see her father, she also had no interest in being associated with Olympus. As far as she was concerned, the place was corrupt. A place she would never want to return to once she was wedded. She did not want to be part of the corruption that forced Hades to the Underworld. If anything, he was a victim of the cruelty her family had inflicted on him.

The civilians worried about Hades return, but the real fear should have been of her father. He would smite many who didn't deserve it, simply because he wielded the power to do such a thing. Both he and her grandfather were not beings she was proud to be related to any longer.

"Not exactly, Mother." Persephone gritted through a smile as she waved to passing relatives crowding the foyer. "I don't favor the way Poseidon shows me affection." She truthfully added, though it wasn't the main reason for not wanting to be on Olympus.

"Oh hush now, he's your uncle whom you only see a few times out of the year." Persephone rolled her cinnamon orbs, continuing down the hall alongside her mother.

Light and airy clouds surrounded Olympus, white fog shielding the blue hue of the sky from the fogged windows. Such a bland place this was to her. There was not much to look at or do aside from interacting with the other Gods and Goddesses here; which she had no intention of doing.

"Persephone, look how big you've gotten!" Persephone heeded the elated tone off to the side.

It was her stepmother and aunt, Hera.

Hera approached, her lengthy brown waves shifting with her movements as she wrapped Persephone tightly in an embrace. "Surely you've found a nice man to marry, with such beauty." Persephone gave an uncomfortable smile to the Goddess of Marriage.

"No. I have no one who I deem worthy enough to take my hand." Persephone lied through her teeth, the statement casting shock across Hera's features. Her thin pink lips formed a worried line, her brows creasing and darkening her baby blue orbs.

"We'll have to fix that, won't we? You are much past the age of adulthood, it's time you found someone. I will speak with Aphrodite, Goddess of Love." Persephone wanted to vomit. She quickly calmed the reflex in her throat and gave a tight smile.

"Thank you, Hera." The entire time, Demeter was casting cold eyes at Hera. It's no secret that the two did not get along. Once close sisters, now fighting for Zeus attention. Hera was the one and only wife of Zeus, while Demeter and many other Goddesses were mere lovers. Nothing more to him. Her mother was always rather jealous; she was not his first or his favorite.

Persephone turned away from the Goddess who wore a floor-length cream dress, and jeweled crown with pride.

She hated her aunt. How could she marry such a monster?

Those who she had once loved, Persephone now saw as nothing but despicable beings.

Finally, Demeter and her daughter neared the throne in which Zeus sat all high and mighty. He sat slightly slouched, a gilded leaf crown tilted on his head of white hair with a beard of the same hue to match his toga. A golden ribbon tied around his waist, keeping the cloth in place.

"Daughter Persephone." He greeted, indifference in his tone. Persephone lowered herself to her knee.

"Father." She acknowledged, uttering nothing more.

"Don't you have something to say to your father, Persephone?" Persephone glanced at her mother, her eyes emotionless.

"I wish to say nothing more. I have nothing to say to him." She bitterly grumbled. Even just knowing he was her father turned her insides unpleasantly.

"That's how you greet our father?" Athena, Goddess of War and Wisdom was at the right hand of her father's throne, raising an angered brow at her sister Persephone clenched her teeth together.

"He deserves nothing more." She hadn't meant for that to leave her lips so carelessly. "Besides it's not as if he cares for me anyway. I don't remember him much from childhood because he was too busy cradling you. It is no secret you are his favorite, so why would I try to earn his love? Not that I want such a thing from him."

"Persephone! That is enough! What has gotten into you?!" Her mother Demeter was horrified, Persephone casting cold eyes to her father.

"I'm just in need of rest after the long trip," Persephone mumbled, her father sharing a similar glare as her.

"Where is your necklace?" Persephone reached up to touch the bareness of her neck where the amulet he had given her for protection used to exist.

A grin darkened her features.

"I lost it while taking a swim in the lake." Persephone rose from her knee, ignoring the whispers she was gaining from the rest of her family. "Now if you'll excuse me, I will be going to my chambers until this visitation is over."

She wasted no time fleeing their presence, to her room, where she planned to remain until her mother beckoned her to return home.

It was a taboo to even mention Hades here in Olympus, but that did not stop Persephone from performing her daily sacrifice to him. She lit candles, made a small shrine from books gathered from the shelf within her room, and removed the humming cicada from her satchel found in the beautiful garden she and her mother had grown here on Olympus

She then stabbed her dagger through the insect.

Once done, she blew out the candles, and that was when the clash of thunder just outside her window startled her. She jumped back with a gasp, the bright light shaking her window.

Heavy droplets soon followed the light, trickling against the windowpane.

"It hasn't rained in Olympus in over three thousand years." The hushed voice passing outside of her door piqued her interest. *"Not after he was gone. You believe he has returned?"*

Persephone rose from the floor, adjusting her earthy toned curls, and moving towards her door where she waited for the footsteps to grow distant.

She cracked her door in the slightest, finding the hallway to be empty, and hushed voices coming from the gathering quarters down the hall. A dim glow peered from beneath the double doors, illuminating the red velvet hall.

Cautiously, she stepped from her room, and shut the door behind her, creeping down the red carpeting towards the room.

She inched closer, pressing her back to the wall, and listening to the chatter carry on from behind the doors.

"I have been informed of Hades return." Zeus' voice boomed with pure wrath, Persephone becoming shaken momentarily. "Worshipers have been praying and begging me to bring life back to their crops and wondering as to what they did to deserve their dying cattle or sick relatives. I know it is his work. Have any of you encountered him?"

There were mumbles of astonishment, none of the Gods of Goddesses having seen nor contacted him for years.

"Hermes?"

As a messenger between both Gods and mortals, and the one who leads the dead to the Underworld, he was a suspect.

"Of course I have, but I go no further than the tunnel of the path the dead walk. I have no choice." He reasoned, which Zeus believed. After all, it was his duty.

"Why would he return to the mortal world? What does he have planned? Are the mortals safe?"

Questions were thrown around, Zeus attempting to answer all of them when he brusquely outburst.

"Silence!" Another roar of thunder sounded over his voice.

"We will not panic about such a minuscule God. If he does not return to the Underworld where he belongs, I will assure his punishment, as well as anyone involved."

Persephone stepped away from the wall, her hand cupping over her mouth as sweat began to bead her blanching skin.

To her, this was frightening news.

She rushed down the hall and returned to her room. She was a flushed mess as she locked her door behind her.

She had to warn him as soon as she returned to the mortal world.

✦

Persephone had found the will to sleep, even with the loud thunder flashing occasionally outside of her window.

She peacefully slept, until her subconscious felt someone watching her, bringing her eyelids to flutter open.

Her bleary vision gazed up in confusion, finding a black shadow hovering over her, vibrant azure irises burning to her sleeping being.

Her sleep filled eyes widened, and just as she had gone to scream, a heavy hand clasped over her mouth.

The figure allowed her wide eyes to focus, finding a familiar presence that brought goosebumps to coat her flesh.

"You wouldn't cause me trouble, would you?" Persephone relaxed in the softness of the bed, her brows creasing as she swatted his hand from her mouth.

"Are you a loon?! You could get yourself killed here." She hissed, Hades shifting to sit on the edge of her bed.

"You appear to be more caring of my life than I." He became amused, Persephone biting back foul words as she quickly sat up in bed.

"How did you even get here, Ha-" Hades put a finger to his lips, and Persephone swallowed his name. "How did you enter Olympus? You've been banned."

He took in her inquisitive countenance, while he mulled over his thoughts and whether the girl was trustworthy enough to tell.

"Hermes and I are very much on good terms. In secret of course. He invited me in so long as I was hidden, though my presence is obvious here." He motioned to the gloomy weather.

Hermes? He went against her father? What a brave soul he was. He might be the only God she had any respect left for.

"I thought I'd pay you a visit considering your father was discussing all the tragedies I've committed in the mortal world." He licked his teeth, leaning in towards Persephone. "I am very much intrigued by your harshness towards your father." A fierce blood rush reddened her face, causing her gaze to cast away.

"I never liked him much." She replied, to which Hades drew his claws under her chin, and brought her saucer-like eyes back to his hooded, viperous ones.

"That much is certain, yet you've become rather hostile towards him recently. I wouldn't have something to do with that, would I, flower girl?" Persephone swallowed roughly, readying to deny his accusations. "It seems you hate your entire lineage. That was also my doing, wasn't it? But you don't hate me like you hate the others, do you?" Persephone closed her gaping mouth, and Hades grinned, his fangs cradling against his bottom lip as he tenderly stroked her brown tresses. "No. Of course not." He answered for her, bringing the sweet-scented girl close enough to breathe against her clenched throat. Persephone clutched the fabric of her bedsheets in anticipation.

"You and I share the same perspective, yet we are meant to be opposite. You are a sweet-scented flower, while I am the poison that rots them away. But you are not just a flower are you, Persephone? You are a poison too." Hades' hand crawled up her dress, Persephone flinching when his claws dug into her thigh. "Aye?"

"Yes." She squeaked, her hand coming up to stroke his shadowed locks. A soft hiss was masked by another crackle of lightning.

"You may love the adorning aroma of flower beds, and it may be embedded in you, but you also like the scent of death that lingers off me, hmm? Is that why you want me to keep coming back?" Hades' hand traveled further up her thigh, pushing her back against the pillows. Her bewildered mien drank Hades in as he hovered just a hair from her lips.

Persephone drew back a few black strands that escaped from their neatly combed state, unsure as to why he was suddenly this intimate. Not so long ago, he barely desired her touch.

That was before she showed her devotion to him. Now that she had plagued herself, and sullied her reputation in secrecy, he was convinced she was nothing like her family.

She was different. She could bring both happiness, and Hell if she desired. Something that intrigued the God who only saw in black and white, life and death. How could she possibly bring both life and death?

"You despise your father. I despise your father. You want to explore elsewhere. So why don't we discuss a compromise; one that will be sure to please the both of us."

Hades traced his claw between her legs, and she sucked in a sharp breath through gritted teeth, Hades pinning her hands over her head as he leaned in, and drew her dress up further, exposing her stomach to his touch.

"And what might that be, Hades?"

Hades brushed his lips over her parted petals and skimmed them over the smooth texture, retaining his grin as he spoke his next words against her.

"A kidnapping."

Chapter Six
FALSE ABDUCTION

"A kidnapping?"

Persephone was stunned at first, the astonishment leading her to be unsure as to how she should respond.

"Yes. A kidnapping." Hades withdrew his touch, allowing Persephone to sit up with the conversation growing serious. "You see, if I were to kidnap you on the grounds of marriage-"

Persephone's brows furrowed, her mouth opening in rebuttal.

"Marriage?"

Hades was completely nonchalant, more annoyed to have been interrupted than anything.

"Marriage, Persephone. Now stop speaking and allow me to finish." Still befuddled, she allowed him to continue in hopes he would clear up her confusion. "As I was saying. If I were to kidnap you for the reason of marriage, that would surely infuriate all the above. It would not only anger Zeus, but your mother. Two whom I dislike very much. It is a possibility that I will be able to settle my vendetta with him, hopefully ending in his death once he tries to retrieve you. And you, well you would get to visit the Underworld, and see another world aside from the one filled with clouds and peonies."

Persephone took the suggestion into consideration, contemplative over his words. Faking both a kidnapping, and a marriage sounded like the excitement she craved. She desired to add excitement to her life and Hades was handing it to her.

It would work out in both their favors.

She truly did want to know what the Underworld was like, how he ran his world. What existed there. It piqued her interest.

"So, you would kidnap me on the grounds of a false marriage? How would we go about committing to this act?"

Hades gazed heavenward and exhaled sharply.

"It truly isn't hard to fake such a thing."

Persephone rolled her cinnamon irises to the ceiling.

"You do realize my father isn't an imbecile, right? He didn't become king of the Gods by being moronic."

Hades curled his lip.

"Yes, I know. But I am no fool either, and I won't allow him to win a second time." Persephone advanced towards him, folding her legs under her as she held the blue flames of his gaze.

"What is your plan, Hades?"

৻৶

Persephone had gone home the next evening, and the two agreed that when the sun would set, they would set their plan into action.

No doubts or fears crept into her thoughts when she heeded his plan, for she longed to be away from this dreadful place she had once called home.

The sun was setting, pink and orange hues painting the mortal sky. She and her mother were in a forest closest to their temple, growing the budding crops. Demeter took care of the wheat stalks used for livestock, while Persephone had told her mother she wanted to take a break and admire the plant life.

"Don't go too far, Persephone." Demeter warned.

Persephone promised she wouldn't venture off, little did her mother know.

Persephone trudged deep into the forest, sounds from the lively town beginning to fade. The bird songs had become chirps of crickets, Persephone halting her stroll when she became surrounded by towering trees, their darkening leaves shading her from sunlight.

Perfect. Now she would impatiently wait for him to return. She tapped her foot against the plush grass, the color dwindling as she began losing sunlight. Flowers began to close for the evening, falling into slumber until the sun would rise again.

She gave an exasperated huff, folding her arms over her chest.

What was taking him so long?

He had told her as soon as the sun would set, he would be here, but has yet to show his face.

"Persephone!" She heard her mother call.

Persephone veered around in the direction of the summon, a frown pouting her lips.

He probably wasn't coming.

Persephone cast her ire-filled attention away from the landscape and turned to find Hades.

"Are you ready, Persephone?" She leaped from against the tree supporting her weight, and any irritation she felt prior had dissipated.

"Of course, I am-"

"Persephone, where are you?" Demeter's shrill had grown closer, Persephone speaking to Hades in a whisper.

"But we must hurry," Persephone concluded, Hades beckoning her over, and forcing her to kneel.

"You understand that once you've committed to this, and our scheme is discovered, you can be cast out of Olympus, or worse."

Persephone cocked her head back up to him as he materialized twine in his grasp to tie her up.

"I do, and I will have no regrets. He will not find out, so long as we assure my hatred for you is believable, just as we disclosed."

Hades knelt, beginning to thread the twine around her

wrists.

Hades tightly knotted the string, bringing her to flinch in discomfort.

"Have you considered binding me a little tighter?"

Hades did as she sarcastically asked, and grinned, drawing up her face.

"Better?"

Persephone returned the snarky beam, resting her being against him.

"Much." Hades moved to her ankles with the bindings, loosely tangling the rope around them. He gripped her arm roughly, and tossed her weight over him, jamming his shoulder into her stomach. Persephone grunted, and squirmed in a poor attempt to gain comfort, however the moment she shifted, she nearly fell over, face first onto the grass with her hands bound behind her.

"Must you be so barbaric? I thought we were pretending!" Her fiery tongue spat, Hades chuckling as he held tightly to her hips.

"Pretend for us, but it must be believable for others." Hades silently stalked through the trees, putting distance between them, and her mother. After a few paces more, he snapped his fingers.

Following the simple action, a crackle of thunder startled her, leading her to cry out. Over her startled shriek, the galloping and howls of horses widened her eyes, Persephone unable to see the chariot before Hades, for she was faced away.

"Good, scream a little louder. I want them to hear you." Hades playfully pinched her hip, earning a yelp from the flower girl draped over his shoulder like a damp rug. Her brunette curls hung over her eyes in a messy manner, the thick locks confiscating her sight.

"You're getting awfully carried away." She dug her knee to his chest, a displeased sound making its way to his throat, and locked behind his sharp teeth.

"Don't make me toss you." Before she could counter his threat, she was thrown into the chariot, Hades gripping her leg harshly, and drawing her to the edge of the seat.

"Ouch!" Persephone winced, Hades lowering himself, so he was leveled with her lips.

"Start making a scene." The young Goddess gaped at him momentarily before she truly began to wail. Kicking her bound legs and pleading for help she didn't need. She squirmed so terribly, she accidentally thrashed her foot to his face, and he hissed.

"Tone it down, would you?"

Angry fire flamed through her roughly pulsing being, her glare burning into him.

"Do you want this to be believable or not?! I'm very confused." Just then, the patter of her mother's steps raced towards their commotion.

Hades threw the hood of his cloak over his blue flaming hair.

Demeter had become panicked. Where had her daughter gone? Where was her scream coming from?

Her wide eyes and perspired skin sticking to her white dress admitted the terror she currently felt.

It brought a leer to Hades' face, his cloaked expression barely visible in the dim light the evening had to offer.

He rapidly faced away, and climbed onto his chariot, gripping onto the reins, and striking the horses.

Demeter called out frantically to the eerie chariot, attempting to dash after them. By then, she had been left with swept up dirt.

"Persephone!" She cried, dropping to her knees. Tears streaked her face, her palms pressed to the dried earth below.

Hades peered over his shoulder, the two moving so fast, they had long surpassed the wandering eyes of any townspeople. They were now moving through the darkened forest, on a path that would lead them directly to the Underworld.

Everything had gone smoothly, just as he desired.

Even though she had been forced to listen to her mother's

doleful cries from the back of Hades chariot, it didn't bother her not one bit.

Her mother was always trying to keep her sheltered, and it appeared she cared more about her image than she did about her own daughter's wanting's.

Persephone sat up, worming her way over to Hades, and blowing an askew lock of hair from her face.

He cast a quick glance at her, drawing the horses to a slow trot.

"Would you like to guide them?" Persephone was stunned into a stupor yet again, so much so, she hadn't noticed her bindings had come undone with a simple stare from Hades.

"I've never led horses. I wouldn't even know where to direct them-" Hades waved off her declining words, passing the reins over to Persephone as he reclined in his seat. He kicked up his feet, and eased himself back, completely relaxed.

"The horses are mine, they know where their home is. All you have to do is whip the reins to speed them up." Persephone held the reins unsurely in her grasp.

She looked at them, her eyes lighting up.

Her first taste of freedom.

She would've never been allowed to do such a thing if she remained with her mother, forced to be a young lady, but that isn't wasn't she wanted. Her life was so constricting. She was a Goddess of flowers, but nurturing nature wasn't fulfilling anymore. She wanted so much more.

Persephone whipped the reins, the leather snapping against the horses, causing them to whinny, and race down the dirt road. The cart nearly toppled over, Hades gripping onto the side of the chariot to stable his once tranquil being. He hollered something about slowing down, but Persephone wouldn't sacrifice that crisp night air rushing against her flesh for anything.

She wanted freedom, and now she had it.

For the first time in her life, she was truly free.

Chapter Seven
THE UNDERWORLD

Hades had taken hold of Persephone's reckless driving, seizing the lead before they arrived at the gates of the Underworld. Persephone squirmed in her seat, eyeing the large black gates in excitement. Even as they blindly charged into the dark unknown, Persephone wasn't afraid. She gripped the seat in excitement, thrill glittering in her cinnamon orbs.

"We're here now?" Flames of blue did very little to light the scene, Hades' glowing indigo irises matching the blazes. They caught sight of Persephone's unruly appearance, her thick curls windblown, dried leaves and twigs weaved into her tresses. Her pupils were dilated, Hades snapping his fingers to allow her more light. Unlike him, she was unadjusted to the near black atmosphere, living in sunlight all her life.

"We are."

With more illumination, Persephone scanned the area, the cave-like surroundings not much to be elated about, yet she was. It was new, a change from her usual scenery.

Hades leaped from the carriage, holding out his hand. Persephone took his scaly textured appendage, into her soft touch hitching up her skirts to cautiously tread out of the chariot.

She took the last step, the beam she wore unwavering.

Her bliss alone could light up this hole, Hades deeming her smile bright enough to do such a thing.

"Are you going to let go of my hand?" Persephone laughed, Hades having not realized he was still holding her silky fingers. He snatched his hand back, clearing his throat, and pulling the collar of his tunic.

"This way." He murmured, facing away from her to move towards the gate leading to the tunnel of souls.

A rumbling growl quaked the ground beneath them, Hades rapidly turning to Persephone who gazed around in confusion.

A giant, three-headed beast lunged from the shadows towards the befuddled girl. Hades rushed over, placing an arm in front of her. The beast barely grazed the ceiling, its massive height looming over them as if they were mere insects.

The muscular beast bared its large canines, bloodied saliva dripping from its snarled mouths. Six red eyes were locked to Persephone as if she were fresh meat, snapping its jaws at her.

"No." He hissed, his eyes becoming slits to warn off Cerberus.

Persephone gasped, Hades mistaking the gesture for shock until she spoke.

"Is that Cerberus? Protector of the gates? What a beautiful creature." She praised, sauntering from behind Hades to near the beast. She outstretched her hand out to pet its snouts, Hades preparing to chastise her.

Cerberus continued to growl, Persephone smiling up at it, holding her hand out in waiting. His monstrosity stifled its threatening snarls, staring in bemusement upon the young Goddess. She giggled, Cerberus lowering its heads to bow before her. It completely rested to the floor, allowing Persephone to stroke them.

"My, my how beautiful are you? Pretty as posies." Hades stood there, his jaw slack in astonishment. Cerberus had never bowed to anyone other than he. Anyone else, they tore the limbs from, but not she.

She terrified them.

"Come along, Persephone. You have much to see." Cerberus remained as they were, Persephone waving to the creature before she ventured forth with Hades. "We will need to travel through the tunnel of souls in order to get to the heart of the Underworld."

The gates were opened, the ear-aching screech trembling the sharp rock so overhead. On each side of the gate, two creatures greeted them, Persephone eyeing the oddities of each. Half goat and half man, walking on hoofs. The other shared the same attributes. They, in turn, ogled her in curiosity as she passed, Hades striding onward. Persephone stayed closely behind, the chilly air of the Underworld offering her the consolation of night. It was only at night that she would lack the warmth of the sun, Apollo allowing Selene a chance to shine her frigid moonlight.

They continued on the stone path, the faint hush of racing water catching her attention. Hints of a metallic odor followed, scrunching her features. She could practically taste the brine on her tongue when she breathed.

Persephone shielded her nose, the pungent scent growing more repulsive as they grew closer.

"What in the world is that awful stench?" Hades stopped once they reached the edge of the path, black liquid rushing over jagged rocks in front of them. The unpleasant fetor radiated from the harsh stream, watering her eyes.

"Decomposed bodies." Hades faced her, a decently sized canoe approaching behind him. Standing hunched, and rowing their transportation was a cloaked hag, old and withering with age. Her gray hair was matted beneath the hood of the cape in which she shielded her hideous features. Persephone was able to make out her crooked tooth and twisted nose; heavy wrinkles crinkling her squinting eyes. "Their blood runs heavily through the waters of the Underworld. The flesh and organs belonging to the wandering souls are drowned here." Just then a bloodied hand clasped around her ankle, startling her. She cried out, staring down into an eyeless cadaver. It groaned, clutching her leg as if she would help pull it from its current misery.

Persephone was stunned stiff, Hades kicking the hand away. He smirked.

"Be careful, all are restless here." He smirked.

Persephone was expecting this much from the Underworld, after all, it was a place of death.

Hades assisted Persephone onto the roomy canoe, seating themselves down as the woman began to row.

Cries, moans, and other painstaking noise filled the river of Styx; however, it didn't bother Persephone much.

"You've lived down here all this time," She commented in awe. A strange pulling sensation beckoned her to this eerie place. "Have you ever wanted to leave?" Her cinnamon orbs glistened awaiting his answer.

Hades pursed his lips in thought.

"Perhaps at one time, yes. Eventually I came to realize that I am a God of darkness. Of misery. This is where I belong." Persephone toyed with the fabric of her dress, frowning at his words.

"You must grow lonely down here, no? Is that why you came to the surface?"

"I do not. I dislike company." His features curled in disgust. "I came to the surface out of curiosity."

"Is that so?" She whispered, a little smile quirking her moue. "Why did you crawl to the human world anyway? What had drawn you there?"

"The golden sunlight. Never had it reached the pits of Hell until you-" Hades caught himself answering the young goddess' inquiries with ease, charmed by those doe eyes of hers. He gritted his fanged teeth.

The Goddess didn't appear to be listening thankfully. Persephone was clinging to the rim of the boat, gazing about at the ghostly souls that rose from the bubbling river, like rising steam. A translucent female emerged from the bloodied river, leaning towards Persephone and pecking her cheek. She dispersed soon after, a cloud of white mist speckling the air.

Persephone touched her cheek, turning to Hades. Her expression was gleeful, and the brightness of her aura must have stirred the undead beings, having not been exposed to gentleness indefinitely.

They approached the tunnel, the hag halting the ore she paddled. The boat skimmed the lip of the stony path, howls of saddened souls swarming the path.

"The tunnel of souls is ahead. Once they're stripped of their flesh, the souls are guided here, where they are cared for by Hermes, or my goat, Demokritos." Persephone wasn't hesitant as she took his hand and pursued his steps, willingly walking amongst the dead.

Blindly they strode, the one source of light igniting the scales burrowed in his blackened arms. Blue flames chased the undead away, Persephone's attention latched to him.

She knew very little of the God, how malicious he could be, or how cunning those claimed him to be. How cruel he had been, and that is why he was never spoken of, but Persephone could not see such traits.

The flames that licked his skin were warm, encasing her own hand. Never did they burn her. *Aside from that one time of course.* He chose not to harm her.

Her hand entwined in his like wild vines, Hades stiffening in her touch. He remained mute, a dim glow at the end of the tunnel drawing near.

Persephone blinked her strained eyes, sheltered in the dark for too long.

Her blurred sights wavered, widening upon the astonishing atmosphere. Her breath hitch in her chest, the ruler beside her leveling close to her ear.

"Welcome to Hell, My Queen."

Chapter Eight
HIS SANCTUM

The teal glow of the water reflected in her cinnamon irises, the cascading crystal liquid flooding into a pond. Bloomed water lilies cluttered the bubbling water, steam rising and mingling with small blue orbs that danced about the lively scenery. Laced around the ledge were clusters of evening primrose, lavender, and moonflowers. The captivating hues of violets, dimmed whites, and soft lapis illuminated the gloominess that was the Underworld.

Her very breath had been stolen in admiration of the scenery.

"You did this, you know." Hades motioned to the floral arrangements and life filled sector of his stony kingdom. Night flowers pushed through the broken rock, sprouting eagerly to stretch towards the darkness.

"Me?"

"Yes. My lovely creatures somehow believed I adored flowers because of that abomination over there." Persephone peered off to where Hades directed. In a shaded area, her straining eyes found a patch of grass bearing dandelion, daisies, and plentiful wild plants. The reddest roses she had ever seen grew amongst them, Persephone's heart soaring seeing the divine beauty.

"Every time I tried to burn them, they'd simply grow back. Your flowers fed off your blinding sunlight, and the blood of the deceased." Persephone was not surprised by this statement in the least. Life and death were not strangers to her. Her mother had always told her that she should never mourn the dead. The dead give new life to the earth, nourishing all plant life, assisting them in their duty. "Because I gave up on eradicating them, these little imps thought I desired more." Hades flicked one of the approaching blue orbs, a high-pitched squeak sounding from it.

More floating cerulean spherules frolicked near, Persephone gasping when one rapidly flew into her line of sight. Persephone's eyes crossed, sheer fascination parting her lips.

The minuscule illumination tittered, others too intrigued by Persephone.

"Is this her? Is this her? Is this her?" Little voices chirped, their mischievous giggling overwhelming. Persephone took a step back from the gathering orbs.

"Yes, yes. This is her, stop pestering." Hades dusted them away like pesky insects, one of the orbs dispersing into a cloud of mist. The tumbling light had changed appearance, morphing into a faerie. She shook her head, her body fluttering about as she attempted to steady her dizzied form. She was a tiny creature; dragonfly wings fluttering rapidly as her large, bug eyes studied the Goddess of Spring. Her lapis shaded eyes resembled that of a fly, minute hexagon shapes making up her sights. Her flesh was a hue of cornflower, her grinning mouth harboring rows of needle-like teeth.

Elation sparkled in Persephone's eyes, having never seen the mischievous creatures in person. She's only heard tales of them.

"Very pretty, very pretty Goddess." She cooed, fluttering up to prop herself on Persephone's shoulder. "Will you be his Queen?"

"Aye." Persephone confidently replied, knowing she would

soon partner to Hades under their agreement to keep her here and anger her father out of spite.

"Will you be a good Queen or a bad Queen?" Before she answered, Hades clasped a hand over her lips, the words lingering on her tongue.

"Be careful with them, Persephone. They're in the Underworld for a reason. None here are of pure heart. They will twist your words."

The faerie leaped from Persephone's shoulder, two more of the creatures showing their true form.

"We wish not to harm the new Queen, Lord Hades!" A second feigned offense, her hand coming over her chest. Hades ignored the creature, taking Persephone's wrist.

"We don't have time to fool around, allow me to show you the remainder of the residence." Persephone left behind the tittering critters, pursuing Hades. She expected for the Underworld to be horrendous. Blood staining the walls, chained prisoners, punishment around every corner, but she was pleasantly surprised. Having been greeted by gloomy scenery that captivated her attentive gaze, she had expected the remainder of the Underworld to be the same, yet it was not.

Glossed black marble covered cracked stone, bones of the dead molding to create furniture added an eerie beauty, obsidian chandeliers, and midnight silk sheets all fed her wonderment.

"This is just my sanctum." He said to the curious Goddess. "The Underworld is far bigger, and it would take days to show you the entirety. Will this do until you are rested?" He inquired, raising his brow to Persephone who was tracing her fingers over the sleek charcoal granite table. Pointed rock of all different sizes covered the ceiling, the natural structure piecing together perfectly amongst the grim interior.

She hadn't expected such a dark place to hold unique beauty.

"It's absolutely stunning." Persephone faced Hades, his paled formed contrasting the dull atmosphere.

"I suppose this part is extravagant, but understand the remainder isn't as lovely. This is the Underworld." Persephone nodded in understanding, the query she wished to ask caught in her throat when the clatter of hooves approached.

"This is Persephone, Zeus' daughter." A gravelly tone acknowledged. "She is our Queen? Have you gone mad? Do you wish to have all of Olympus to smite you?" The clack of their steps stopped at her side, Persephone finding a horned man at her side, his chest covered in fur as well as his lower half that resembled a grazing animal.

"Quiet you goat. They've already done so, what worst could they do?" Hades reached for Persephone, his hand cupping her chin so that she looked at Demokritos. "Besides, her mother is sure to sob over missing this youthful face. Wouldn't you?" Persephone tucked a curl behind her ear, allowing the creature a clear look to her warm appearance. "And Zeus will be angry I'm sullying a daughter of his,"

Persephone interjected then, tearing from Hades.

"I don't think he will care much. He doesn't enjoy my presence."

"Oh, dearest Persephone, you have much to learn about your father. It doesn't matter if he cares for you or not. The sheer thought that I have my hands on something of his alone will boil his blood."

Persephone frowned, Hades noticing her displeasure, so quickly he changed the conversation.

"If you're going to be my wife, you will dress accordingly, no?" Persephone perked up, Hades continuing his thought. "A Queen needs to make a good first impression." He teased, Persephone giggling. She enjoyed that the two were scheming. Being a good child all her life, she was thrilled to have finally escaped the mind-numbing cycle of living to please those on Olympus.

"Can we assist, Lord Hades? Can we, can we?" A blue orb had traveled through the shadowed hall, manifesting into her faerie form. She fluttered about, wiggling her rump in glee.

"No. I don't need you making a wreck of my bride. I will allow you to dress her, and she will return to me as a frog, or with cropped hair."

"Never!" The faerie squirmed, an impatient squeak sealed behind her lips. "Queen Neráida desires to meet her, she will make her beautiful."

Hades then pinched the faerie's wings together, holding her inches from his face. "No. She will certainly not be acquainting herself with Neráida. Neráida is the most troublesome of the lot of you." The faerie scrunched her features, fighting to get out of his grasp.

"She is not! She's a very good Queen. Very good!" Hades exhaled heavily, setting the faerie free.

"Fine. Dress her, but be quick about it. She's certainly tired after the trip and is in need of rest." He let her loose, the faerie dusting her little garments made up of flower petals. "Persephone, follow the imp to their Queen. She rarely comes to visit the Underworld, but when she does it's because she is here to cause a disturbance." The faerie tugged on her finger, urging her to accompany them.

Persephone glanced over her shoulder at Hades in an unsure manner, Hades waving her forward. "Go on. They will show you the faerie realm." The faerie tugged her forward impatiently, glitter dust fanning from her wings. A blinding white light brought Persephone to turn her head, her attention cast away.

"Come! She beckons you, Goddess!" More blue orbs pushed her forward, and one would believe that a critter of their size would be weak in comparison to her. That was far from the truth. They were rather strong, ushering her towards the light, and tugging her limbs.

Persephone glanced behind her once more, Hades collected as they dragged her forward. His arms folded over his chest, his shoulders relaxed as if he trusted them to return her as she was.

The Spring Goddess moved forward to the light, easing the tension she caused the faeries. She placed a bare foot into the

JASMINE GARCIA

warm luminescence, the tingling illumination inviting her forth to be completely consumed.

Chapter Nine
QUEEN NERÁIDA

olden grass pricked her soles, the orange glow of the setting sun casting silhouettes of trees to stretch athwart the field. The melodic twitter of singing birds flying overhead, and the soothing chatter of wildlife brought the comfort of home.

"Goddess of Spring!" A dandelion orb skipped amid the numerous blue lights, her form morphing into a yet another faerie. Flames covered the entirety of her, her hair flickering like the wick of a lit candle. Unlike the blue faeries, her skin was a pale cream, save for the distinct glow that enveloped her. Her eyes were two black holes, like two marks burned into her skull. "Neráida eagerly awaits you!" The blue faeries pushed the blazing faerie, taunting snickers cast her way. She instantly flamed orange, the flames that she bore intensifying. One of the cerulean faeries liquified. Her turquoise skin was as translucent as the calmest river, shooting water at the blazing faerie. A hiss of smoke startled Persephone, the flaming faerie drenched and shielding her nude appearance now that the flames had dithered.

"Neró, Pyre. Is this any way to behave in front of our guest?" Emerging from the shadows of autumn trees, a woman stalked over. Her eyes were as green as the thriving seedlings, her sleek, waist long mane mirroring a starless night sky. Her pallid complexion shared semblance to winters first snow, unblemished by the footprints of forest creatures. A crown of twining twigs bearing leaves and budding flowers weaved through her silky tresses, exposing her elvish ears.

"Apologies, Queen Neráida!" The faeries cried, Neráida moving to the dripping wet faerie. Cradling the quivering critter in her hands, a warm radiance eluded from her palms, enveloping the faerie to dry her. Once more the sunny faerie burst with flames, fluttering ashes from her flaming wings. Neráida set her down, turning her attention to a stiff Persephone, who was stunned by her beauty.

"Persephone," Her name was a gentle breeze that left the Queen's rose-red lips. "How surprising that Hades has chosen a vibrant maiden such as yourself." Her airy voice had Persephone choking on words.

What should she say? Should she have bowed to her? Compliment her? What was acceptable to say to the Queen of Faeries?

A lightweight laugh pinked Persephone's cheeks, Neráida's warm beam reminding Persephone of daylight, something she didn't expect to see from the supposedly mischievous Queen.

"Hades has painted you to be this noisy, flirtatious girl, yet you are innocent and silent. Like a doe." If Persephone could, she too would have lit aflame, similar to the faerie watching the two interact.

"I certainly am not either. What other lies has that snake said of me?" She snipped, Neráida merely silencing her chortles to a simper.

"I see it now. In your rage, skulls dance in your eyes. Naughty girl indeed." The Queen bid for Persephone to follow. "He speaks much of you. He doesn't even realize it." She sighed, shutting her eyes and pinching the bridge of her nose, tilting her head heavenward. "He used to be so quiet, now he is never quiet. Quite the pest he's become."

Persephone smiled slightly upon hearing he's spoken of her.

She trailed Neráida deeper into the forest. Ahead of her, a throne carved into a tree resided amongst the golden grass, and yellow hued flowers reflecting the light of the setting sun.

Neráida sat in her throne, orbs of all colors, no longer just blue and gold, causing Persephone's eyes to flitter about dizzyingly.

"Oh excuse them. They won't be a bother, will they?" Persephone quickly shook her head. "Good. This is their home after all." Neráida held out her hand, a red orb sitting in the center of her palm. It morphed into a red fleshed faerie, all his features various shades of red.

"This is a healer faerie, they bear the name of Aíma. He and his faerie tend to the wounded, whether it'd be animal or man. Or he can inflict illness or injury depending on his mood." She stroked his head with her thumb. "The blue faeries that resemble insects are water faeries, Neró, common near the aquatic area as you've seen in Hades' kingdom."

"And then there are the Pyre. They create fire and light the forests at night. You wouldn't be able to tell them apart from a flame if you don't look closely enough. As you have seen, their flames change color." Neráida relaxed into her throne. "I would be listing their kind endlessly, so we best leave it at that for now."

A Neró approached and tugged at the hem of her dress, pleading with Persephone to sink into the grass. Persephone did as the antsy faerie wished, numerous hues joining her to play with her brunette curls.

"Be nice to her." Neráida's airy tone commanded, before returning her attention to Persephone. "So, you are to be Queen of the Underworld. That won't be an easy position, though considering your fiery character, I'm sure you will adjust nicely. Even so, I thought you may like some guidance."

Persephone, she still believed this to be a trick. She wasn't truly going to be queen. He just wished to use her to anger Zeus, were none of them aware?

Before she had a chance to interject, Neráida began speaking.

"Arachne, come. Stitch this girl a more fitting garment for rest." Upon command, a woman arachnid lowered herself from a tree, her web easing her eight legs to the ground. Arachne, a woman who was punished by Athena for weaving better than she, stood before her, half spider, and half woman, cursed to forever weave. Challenging the gods was never a good idea.

"Y-You're here in the Underworld?" Persephone stammered in befuddlement.

Arachne's blonde curls framed her sharp features, the peach flesh of her upper half blending into the brown of her abdomen.

"Yes, after your sister turned me into this abomination, I occasionally visit the Underworld." Persephone had a feeling that Arachne wouldn't do any favors for her family. Many disliked them, and she couldn't blame the victims. Persephone was sure her whereabouts would remain secret.

Arachne began grasping shadows as if they were silk, snatching them from trees, faeries, flowers, even weaving part of her own shadow into the garment.

"Don't worry, I have no quarrels with you. Hades is kind to me, so it is only polite to dress his maiden suitably." Silently, she continued her endeavor, animals creeping from the shaded areas she had begun to expose. They were all creatures of oddities. Three-eyed rabbits, two-headed lizards scampering about, Persephone even spotted a headless deer, surely a sufferer of Artemis.

Once Arachne began to weave her creation, the animals settled to nest amongst them, and the faeries sewed flowers into Persephone's hair. That was when Neráida started to give her advice on ruling as a Queen.

"First and foremost, you must rule ruthlessly; punish those who doubt your power."

Neráida spoke for hours, giving Persephone insight on what it meant to be a Queen, however, Persephone failed to heed most of it since the faeries were playfully humming, and giggling in her ears. They were awfully entertained with her hair, dressing the curls in so many flowers she was certain she had a whole garden in her hair.

"How is this Neráida?" Arachne crept to the Faerie Queen, holding up a silky garment. Neráida admired it, taking the material between her fingers, then looking to Persephone.

"I think this is suitable for her. Let's see how Hades will like it." Neráida snapped her fingers and suddenly, Persephone was thrown into another scene. Her head spun, Persephone stumbling to gain her footing.

Cold slate was padded beneath her struggling steps, the tap of shoes ricocheting off the bare walls. In her peripheral vision, she caught sight of a canopy bed, midnight silk draped over it.

"Persephone, I assume Neráida grew tiresome of y-" His phrase cut off, Persephone straining to focus her gaze. Hades' dark form was propped near his altar, the three figures of him finally settling into one.

Once steady, Persephone found his indigo eyes seared to her, his brows creased, his lips parted slightly.

Persephone self-consciously picked at her appearance, touching her loose curls and dusting her shadowed dress...her dress. She hadn't been wearing a black dress prior to being returned. Persephone's fingers entangled in her curls. Weren't flowers braided into her hair?

She caught sight of herself in her reflection behind Hades, a mirror of dark glass revealing her appearance.

A floor length gown loosely framed her curves, the long sleeves bearing ruffles on the cuffs. Her brunette tresses fell in ringlets over her shoulders, framing her gentle features.

Hades caught himself slacked jawed and quickly averted his attention, clearing his throat.

"You're ready for bed then I presume?" Persephone knew her appearance was adorning considering Hades' shy actions.

"Very much so, I'm exhausted." Persephone huffed, giving a little stretch. "You're forcibly my husband now, that's what the others seem to believe." Hades watched her amble to his bed, drawing back the silk curtains. "So you ought to keep up the act, no?" Hades' demeanor had shifted, his venomous teeth flashed in a snarky grin.

"I suppose so. Well? Are you going to get into bed, or should I assist you?"

Persephone lowered herself into his bed, the soft sheets caressing her heated skin.

"Oh no, I'm too frightened of you. I will be obedient tonight, Lord Hades." Hades removed his cloak, draping the fabric neatly over his arm.

"I hope you don't mind, little Persephone. I sleep bare." Persephone blushed then, rendered speechless, and thus losing the playful banter between the two. "I was only jesting." He purred, tipping up her chin to fully examine her flustered countenance.

Persephone sobered up her bashfulness rather quickly, her lips quirked into a half smile.

"You shouldn't tease a lady like that, Lord Hades." Persephone slipped beneath the ebony fabric, Hades standing at the bedside, still amused by her witty response.

"You're awfully foul, Goddess of Spring." Hades chuckled, he too climbing into bed beside the maiden.

"That is because I've been on your arm for too long. You've tainted me." Her brown curls scattered over the feather filled pillows, her cinnamon irises locked with the drapery overhead.

"I can neither prove nor deny that." The flames in the room dimmed upon Hades' command, leaving a soft hue of blue to lantern the spacious room. The bed sunk in, Hades settling in beside her, keeping his distance.

Silence enveloped the pair, Persephone resting a hand on her midsection to count the breaths that would make her drowsy.

Her eyes fluttered closed, succumbing to the exhaustion of tonight's events.

She was here in the Underworld, laying in bed next to the King of the Kingdom. It felt like a dream, none of the events yet settled in.

Her mother was a distant thought. Persephone was angry even with her, although she hadn't thought about the burden she would bring upon her loving mother, and the chaos she would cause on Olympus in the search for her.

Dream or not, Persephone minded it not one bit.

They all deserved to suffer for what they had done to him.

Each and every one.

Chapter Ten
LOSING A CHILD

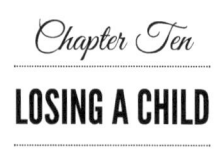

The susurrate of withering leaves clinging to trees fell over the field in which she trekked. Miles of wilting flowers swayed against the weak gust of wind, rustling the crumbling petals. The dried plant life lacked color, hues of unlively gray covering human lands.

Everything was beginning to die.

Demeter took another exhausted step, the crunch of a withered wheat stalk crisp beneath her sandal.

Circles of the darkest storm clouds ringed around her eyes, her skin drained of its tanned hue, reverting to a pigment resembling that of a corpse. Pink stained the whites of her eyes, the heaviness of stones weighing on her chest.

Demeter slumped into the dead field, her short brunette hair askew, the damp earth staining her fair cheeks. Her fingers fisted the dead grass, pushing herself to her feet.

She had to find her daughter. Someone had snatched her from the field while her innocent child was harmlessly exploring. What monstrosity could do such a thing? She had done no wrong.

The Goddess of Harvest took a couple of pitiful steps before her knees gave way once more returning her to the soil.

She was far too exhausted. Her body begged for rest, relentlessly searching for two days and nights, to no avail. Not a trace of her beloved girl was left behind. She had vanished.

Her eyes glossed over, a choked sob dusting up a cloud dried dirt. How could she have been so careless as to not protect her daughter? She should have done more. She should've allowed her to live her life up in Olympus as opposed to here where filthy humans would sully her.

Tears licked Demeter's soiled complexion, her shaking shoulders of stifled sniveling soon becoming vociferous.

Her sobbing curled the wilting vegetation, depriving them of life. The sky grayed, all the land hearing the heart aching cries of a mother without her child. The woeful weeping reached the heavens, summoning a bright ball of golden light that squinted her swollen sight.

Hermes witnessed the crumpled form of Demeter, quickly running over to assist. The golden messenger embraced her, sitting her being upright.

"Demeter, why do you cry so? What troubles you Goddess of Harvest? Why do you revoke all life from this world?" Hermes inquired, peering around at the dried greenery, trees deprived of fruit and leaves. All were brown with death.

Demeter continued to blubber, shielding her face from him.

Her daughter couldn't have been taken far. She just had to keep looking. Demeter thought about walking in circles once again, coming up empty day after day. She couldn't keep this up.

Finally, Demeter accepted the circumstances, her puffy eyes locking with Hermes once she dropped her hands from her face.

"Someone has stolen Persephone. I've searched high and low but cannot find her." Her hoarse voice admitted weakly, the horror of Hermes expression came with him tugging the woman to her feet.

"We must speak to Zeus. Quickly now, we must go!" He ushered her up. Demeter didn't want to bring the problem to Zeus, however, she was desperate, and this was his daughter too.

Compliantly, Demeter accompanied Hermes, the two vanishing in the violent gust of wind carrying dead leaves.

※

Demeter hadn't cared much for her appearance despite the looks of distaste cast her way by the other Gods as she strode down the gilt hall. Her brunette curls were in disarray, her white gown stained in mud, her pale skin also holding the earthy substance. Sadness swelled her deep brown orbs, clear tears streaking her face.

Demeter wiped mucus from her nose using the back of her hand, Hermes guiding her through the extravagant crowd.

Hermes burst through the front doors of Zeus' residence, astonishment visible on the faces of all. Other goddesses sat on the arms of his throne, gushing over him, feeding him fruit.

"Zeus, Ruler of Olympus." Zeus raised his brow in inquiry at their abrupt interruption, unsure as to why Demeter was here when she had recently returned to the human world. Or why her stunning looks were in disarray.

Hermes bowed, Demeter remaining as she was, staring off into the distance.

"This is a matter of urgency, I have just been informed that your daughter, Persephone, Goddess of Spring has been stolen." Zeus straightened in his throne, rising from his seat. All eyes were on them.

"Stolen? By whom?" His voice boomed.

Hermes looked to Demeter, Demeter opening her mouth only no words left. She tried again, her utterance strangled in her windpipe.

"I don't know." Demeter covered her mouth, breaking into sadness once more. Zeus approached her, taking the trembling woman in his grasp.

"Hush now, Demeter. It will be fine." He hugged her in an effort to soothe her tears. Nothing could possibly coddle her distressed cries. Naught but the return of her daughter, safely in her arms.

After rumors of Hades visiting the mortal world, the Gods were anxious, and reasonably so. All he brought with him was misery.

Zeus' lip curled in revulsion.

That serpent tried to kill him, and steal his throne, but he would never allow that to happen again.

He was always trying to steal things that were not his since the pair was younger. He and Poseidon were forced to live amongst that snake, Zeus deeply regretting saving his brother. He was the black sheep of the family. As far as Zeus was concerned, he was the dirt beneath his shoe.

Hades brought nothing but plague and misery to both worlds, leaving Zeus to cast him to the Underworld once he helped dethrone Cronus. He was unworthy to exist on Olympus.

Zeus caressed Demeter's mussed locks, his emotionless tone beckoning his henchmen.

"Gather yourselves in search for my daughter. Search all worlds for her." Zeus ordered, keeping his snowy gaze locked to the wall afore him. "None will rest until she is found."

Chapter Eleven
UNUSUAL MORN

*S*he expected the shine of the morning sun cutting into the slits of her half-opened eyes, drowsy, and yearning to return to slumber. She waited for her mother's screech to beckon her from the warmth of her bedding, scolding her to rouse and dress for their routine of catering to nature.

However, not a peep was heard.

Alarmed, Persephone jolted upright.

Having her eyes partially closed, she failed to see the form that loomed over her slumbering being.

Their heads collided, Persephone wincing, while the being that hovered growled as a dog would.

Persephone rubbed her head, blinking open her blurry sights to catch the predator. She too, held her face, a snarl curling her lips. Her nose jewelry sparkled against the faint blue flames that clung to the walls, her cocoa pigmented skin shimmering bronze under the faint indigo luminance. Six lengthy braids were tight to her scalp, the remainder of the tightly braided tendrils carrying silver beading. She was unclothed, Persephone scampering back to the head of the bed. She had nearly fallen, almost taking the drapery with her if the woman hadn't clutched her leg and dragged her back.

Persephone's eyes were wide, her breathing heavy when she caught a glimpse of sharp teeth within the mouth of her captor. Two rows that could tear through flesh.

"I came to assure your safety, and this is how I am repaid? First, you steal my place beside Hades, and now you can't even uphold respect for me? I am Protector of the Gates, I do not deserve such treatment from a-" Persephone's body relaxed, realizing that she was merely frightened by a shadow. A harmless creature sitting curled on her knees, wiping crimson from her nose.

"Cerberus?" Her brows creased apologetically, clutching the silk sheets beneath them. So this was their human form.

Cerberus glared at Persephone, the Goddess of Spring quickly sharing the same heated stare. Fire blazed in her cinnamon irises, huffing a sharp breath.

"Why were you so close? It is not my fault you cannot understand personal space."

"I was trying to adjust your appearance so that you looked presentable for Lord Hades return." Cerberus smeared the droplets of blood along the back of her hand, eyeing her from head to toe. "Well. As presentable as I could make you since I have naught much to work with." Persephone grit her teeth, a fierce blush staining her tanned skin. "He wouldn't want to come back to a slobbering maiden, hair askew. But I suppose it makes sense that some ungrateful Goddess brat would scold me for my attempts."

The two were at a standstill, and although guilt ate at Persephone, she knew in order to survive here, she needed to be ruthless from the start.

Persephone crawled over, roughly gripping Cerberus' jaw. She forced the creature to face her, Persephone's lethal countenance enough to pale the ferocious creature.

"I am Queen of the Underworld. You will not dare to utter such insults to me again."

Cerberus locked their jaw, slacking their posture in defeat.

When Persephone withdrew, her hands shook. She managed to climb out of bed, straightening out her gown. "Leave." She simply commanded. "I don't need a disrespectful dog guarding me."

The words tasted foul on her tongue. Continuously, she had to remind herself she couldn't show weakness here. She needed to be firm.

"Where would you like me to go?"

"Anywhere but here." Persephone snipped, approaching the vanity.

The patter of their bare feet began to fade, Persephone releasing the breath she was holding in her quivering lungs. She was clutching the chair afore her, suddenly realizing the chair was completely covered in a garden of beautifully colored floral arrangements. Shrubbery made up the back and arms of the chair, as well as the frame for the mirror, skulls sitting on either side of the vanity. Black roses were laced through them. Persephone was astounded by the beautiful pieces that didn't exist last night. At least she didn't recall them.

"Very nice. I see you're properly reprimanding Cerberus as needed. Sometimes they can be very loose with their tongues. Even with me."

Persephone jumped when she caught his shadow in the reflection, spinning around to greet Hades.

"I-I hadn't meant to be so harsh. I just won't tolerate them speaking down to me...if they do it, then others will too."

"That's right." He tipped up her heart-shaped face. A fanged smile, paired with his glowing indigo eyes left her speechless. "Such a quick learner." He brushed his scale covered knuckles over her cheek, Persephone remaining still beneath his cold touch. He dragged his playful gaze away, motioning his claws to the mirror. "The set was a gift from Queen Neráida." He patted the shrub chair, wincing, and rapidly snatching back his hand. He cursed under his breath, holding his bleeding finger to the blue flame that lit the room.

Persephone noticed the shrubbery sprouted thorns, the Goddess giggling. She placed her hand on the chair, and the plant life became docile, a few daisies blooming.

"If you mistreat them, they will mistreat you. Just like a rose uses her thorns to prick those who wish to pluck her, other plant life will do the same." Hades licked the black liquid that oozed from his finger, his forked tongue hissing.

"I care not for such ugly things. If it were up to me I'd burn them all."

Persephone frowned, casting her sights away from him.

Hades saw that his statement had saddened her, sighing, and lifting her attention to him once more. "But I will not touch a petal so long as you are here."

Persephone's glossy eyes stared upon him unsurely, her pout a sign that she was not convinced.

Hades clutched her hands, her small fingers becoming fists when he drew them to his chest. "Nothing you create will perish here. All that is conjured by your hands will be protected."

Persephone gave him a glittering smile then, Hades quickly becoming flustered, and dropping her hands.

He cleared his throat, loosening the tie of his cape. "She also had another dress stitched for you." Hades grasped a dress draped over his altar, the garment resembling the red of pomegranate. He handed her the cloth, turning his back. "Someone is beckoning. Get dressed, and I will return."

Once gone, Persephone stared agape at the garment, unsure as to what the threads were made of this time. It was soft but carried a pungent aroma. Like fruit.

She slipped out of the nightwear, and into the beautiful gown. The dress had a collar that latched around her neck, connected to the bodice covering her chest and torso. Her shoulders were left exposed, and though they were bare, the long sleeves continued to the wrists. At her waist was a ballooned skirt, a very flattering dress for her figure.

Familiar giggling stiffened her, little orbs of varying colors bobbing in the reflection.

"Such pretty hair." They cooed.

Persephone groaned internally, knowing the little creatures would make a mess of her, but she did not argue. They were not being malicious, and so she sat in the plush array of flowers the gifted chair offered, letting the faeries do as they pleased.

In a matter of minutes, Persephone found herself staring at a surprisingly lovely look. They hadn't mussed her hair this time, her truffle brunette waves were combed, two strands closest to her face pinned back by the skull of a bird. Her lips were stained a maroon color, the shade of a dying rose.

Persephone thanked the faeries, one pecking her cheek.

She flinched, for it burned. It was no shock when she noticed it was a Pyre that singed their lips to her, their little flames dancing about.

So excited on how adorning she appeared in this fashion, she was eager to flaunt her looks to her formidable, yet pretend husband.

"Lord Hades!" She called, stumbling into a pair of glossy ruby shoes the faeries shoved in her path. The glassy texture sparkled as if the pair contained stars from the human world.

Through the halls she ran, holding up her dress to prevent herself from clumsily tripping over the ruffles.

She spotted brilliant light at the end of the hall, Persephone following it to the foyer of his sanctum. "Hades, how darling do I loo-"

Abruptly, a hand was harshly clasped over her eyes when she entered, pitch black blinding her. She gasped, her back hugged tightly to a firm being. It was silent.

Gradually, hissing filling the fearsome stillness. Rapid flickers could be felt against her cheeks, the unknown sensation tensing the Goddess.

"Ah, Persephone. Goddess of Spring. What a pleasure to meet your acquaintan-*hiss*."

Chapter Twelve
MEDUSA'S MESSAGE

"Would you truly believe I'd turn your beloved bride to stone?" Tedious steps were heard stalking away, the peppering touch on her flushed cheeks, fleeing. "I wouldn't dare."

"As if I'd believe such tales." The deep utterance belonged to Hades, his words creeping down Persephone's spine.

"Now, why would I wish to harm her? I am merely here to announce that the search for her has begun."

Persephone cringed upon hearing this.

So soon? What if they found her quickly? What then? They could easily just come and snatch her away. Is that what Hades wanted? Just to poke a sleeping dog, and unleash its wrath?

"And why would you be interested in sharing such things with me? You must want something in return."

"Hades. I've never betrayed you. If anyone has hurt you, it is those barbaric Olympians. Just as they hurt me. Poseidon is part of that search party, and you know how much I despise that filthy fish man. Athena as well, considering she turned me into this monstrosity," She released a heavy exhale. "But that's not your concern. Poseidon is. Poseidon has caused us both pain. A common ground between us."

Hades released the constricting hold around Persephone, lowering his hand from her eyes.

Persephone blinked, her blurred vision struggling to adjust to the scene portrayed.

In front of her, an outline of a pallid green figure awaited. Persephone rubbed her sights, gasping when she witnessed snakes gawking at her. She took a startled step back into Hades, Hades holding her shoulders consolingly. The silvery serpents slithered about where her silky tresses once were, her viperous topaz slits cast to the ground, not out of shame, but out of respect for the new Queen's life.

Her skin was pigmented a beautiful sage, a sheen of mercury sparkling her complexion. Scales patched parts of her body; her shoulders, her thigh, her left hand, part of her face. The inconsistency was an oddity that added to her beauty. Many would see her as horrifying, but Persephone did not. She had heard the foul tale of what Athena had done to her after she and Poseidon had defiled the Goddess' shrine.

"Medusa." Persephone's airy voice acknowledged.

"God-*hiss* of Spring, how kind of you to mention my name. Not many wish to speak it."

"I have no fear of you. I am not like those cowardice beings."

Medusa kept her eyes cast off to the side, a fanged grin lighting her features.

"You seem to have been startled when Hades unveiled your eyes."

"I was merely astonished is all. I hadn't expected you." Persephone insisted, folding her arms over her chest, blood rushing to her cheeks.

"It must be a shock to meet so many villainous creatures at once. With the stories they spin in Olympus, I'm surprised you aren't fleeing."

Persephone scrunched her nose in displeasure at the accusation.

"I only fear their ignorance."

Hades sighed heavily behind her, his breath tickling her nape. He dropped his hands from her shoulders, moving towards Medusa.

"If what you say is true, I must keep her hidden for a while. They mustn't know she's here just yet." Hades looked to Persephone, the Goddess blinking her doe orbs.

"How arousing, letting them sweat under the desperation of finding their sweet, sweet daughter." Medusa purred, her silky tone becoming light cackles. She traced her fingers under his chin, drawing his face to her. She cocked her head, her lips lingered over his. "You're going to take her from them, just as they took the throne from you? How cruel of you to include an innocent girl in your quarrels."

Hades snatched from her, Persephone rubbing her arm, and her bashful sights cast to the floor.

She couldn't forget that's all this was. An agreement to enrage her father. A little escape from their worlds.

"Persephone isn't as innocent as you'd believe. Now come, flower;" He directed to Persephone. "I will take you elsewhere until the search party loses hope." Persephone tread forward, clasping the clawed hand he held out to her. "Medusa, you may wait until my return." Medusa rolled her eyes. Just then, an unfortunate creature walked into the room carrying a platter. Her snakes snapped in the direction of the intruder, her topaz eyes locking to her prey.

Instantaneously, the servant stilled, his hideously deformed being solidifying to stone. Like a grotesque statue, he stood, Persephone gasping in awe.

Medusa shut her eyes, giving Hades an apologetic chuckle.

Hades merely exhaled, whipping his hand upright to raise black smoke from the ground.

Persephone squeezed her eyelids shut, clutching onto Hades when a gust of wind swept them elsewhere.

Persephone was unsteady on her feet, the ground feeling as if it were still reeling beneath her long after they settled. The chirping of birds brought her gaze to flutter open, Persephone's white knuckles still clinging to the Lord of the Underworld.

"Back already?" The calming voice that resembled trickling water inquired, Persephone guiding herself to stand erect.

Queen Neráida waited, her brow sternly raised. Her faeries of all colors surrounded, prancing about.

"She needs to be kept hidden for a while."

"To leave an unwed Queen so early isn't proper, Hades. Regardless of your tasteless plots, take her happiness into consideration. She is a Goddess, not some plaything for your feud." Neráida reprimanded, her cold scrutiny glued to Hades.

Persephone's stomach turned, and she shifted uncomfortably although Neráida's anger was directed to Hades.

"She understands her place here. She knows perfectly well that this is simply a skewer in her father's back-"

"She's still but a young girl Hades-"

"Do not project your loveless life onto her. She is content with what was given. Now, keep her hidden until my return." Neráida marched forward prepared to snatch Hades' cloak when he dispersed from the world of faeries. The little orbs that once frolicked around Neráida made themselves scarce in her rage.

"That imbecile!" She stomped her foot.

Abruptly, she remembered Persephone, her vexed features melting away when they witnessed her. "You haven't consumed anything in that dreadful hole, have you?"

Persephone shook her head.

In fact, she hadn't had a bite since before she had left for the Underworld. She had been too wrapped in nerves to properly eat. She couldn't even recall what she had eaten last.

"Good. You don't need to remain with that simpleton. You still have a chance to leave."

Persephone wrung her fingers, averting her attention to the steady flowing stream adjacent to them.

"I am not offended by his behavior. I chose to come here, it was not against my will. Only for show. I knew what was to become of me here, and as Hades said; I am content with the experience of leaving the blue sky, and beaming yellow light behind."

Neráida stepped forward, taking her hands.

"You are a Goddess. A Queen. Do not settle for nothing less than what you're worth."

Persephone looked to Neráida, concern knitting her brows.

"You deserve far more than he intends to give you. All the kingdom and power over it will not quench your desires. Your adventure will soon end, and you will find yourself yearning for something more, something he cannot give you, my Queen." Neráida gently stroked Persephone's untamed curls, her pale touch lingering over the young Goddess' cheek. "It is something you cannot have here, and that is not something you should live without for an eternity. You are not here for punishment."

Persephone was unable to find meaning in Neráida's speech; and so she nodded, utterly dumbfounded.

Just then, Persephone's stomach grumbled, Persephone holding a hand to her noisy belly.

Neráida laughed, wrapping an arm around the Goddess' shoulder.

"Why don't we go and fetch you something to eat? We are not within the Underworld, so you are safe to eat whatever you crave without fear of imprisonment." Queen Neráida guided Persephone alongside her, the little spheres of color returning to prance around them. "And might I say, you look so lovely. Red is suiting for you."

Hades returned to his sanctum, Medusa now contently seated upon his table. In her hand, she held a glass of wine she helped herself to.

"Why are you still here? Begone with you. If they're truly in search of her, it's just a matter of time before they come here."

The moment he spoke, a sharp set of whimpers followed defending growls, leading him to glare at the doorway.

Cerberus rushed into the dining area, no longer in their female form. Instead, a masculine physique took place. Their tanned skin was perspired, clinging to the wall with bloodied hands. Heavy breaths laced their warning.

"Lord Hades, they've entered the Underworld."

Hades cursed under his breath.

"Medusa, leave now. I don't need your slippery tongue spoiling my plans."

"I will leave at my leisure." Medusa took another sip of her drink, Hades prepared to banish her from his sight.

Just then, two pairs of urgent steps entered the room.

"Apologies for the damage to your puppy, but it was in my way." Hekate strode in, Hermes at her side.

"Cerberus, that's enough. I will handle this." Hades ordered without removing his indigo scorn from Hekate.

Cerberus was not to blame for the intruder, for Hekate held a piece of the Underworld with her. She could not be cast out. She would not be cast out. A piece of this domain belonged to her.

Hekate the Goddess of Witchcraft stood afore him, her three bodies representing all she stood for. Three paths, Heaven, Earth, and the Underworld. One of the strongest Goddesses that existed for she could persevere in any setting. Back to back, they stood, watching all around her.

Hekate moved towards Hades, her shimmering black curls bobbing beneath her deep violet cloak. Since she carried three forms for each world, facing him currently, she was embellished in her hellish attire. Her earthly form; composed of dull fabrics blended in with human society, a torch in her left hand. The other form composed from the heavens wore an extravagant white gown, her locks pinned up beneath a golden band, two curls framing her face, while she held a torch in her right hand. Hades just thanked all the Underworld that it was only one pair of eyes glaring at him with distaste instead of three pairs.

"Have you heard that Persephone, Goddess of Spring has gone missing?" Medusa watched in silence, sipping her drink as they all waited for Hades to give his answer.

A coy smile curled his mouth, raising a brow at Hekate.

"Has she? What a shame."

"She had gone missing the day after your apparent appearance on earth, and Olympus. I find that rather odd, no Hermes?"

Hermes, who was silent since arrival regrettably dipped his head. Hades could tell Hermes didn't wish to go against him, but as the messenger between Olympus and the Underworld, he could not pick sides.

"You heard it from Hermes himself. Even he is suspicious of you." All three beings then squinted at him. "All of us are." They said in sync.

"Of course, you'd choose to cling to some silly idea that I'd want Demeter and Zeus' daughter. An outcry for sure. All of you are desperately grasping at straws because none of you know where the girl went."

"I bet you stalked her like the predator you are." Her thunderous voice accused, violet electricity crackling in her fists.

Hades scoffed, tilting his head back in laughter. "How delusional you all are. What use would I have for this little rabbit, hmm?"

"Because you're a vile, twisted man, and live for nothing more than the misery of others."

Hades lifted his hands in surrender.

"Alright, you've got me. Uncovered my true intentions. I took Persephone, and ravished her. I couldn't resist the sweet smell of flowers, and had to have her all to myself!" He exclaimed lunging at the Goddess who hadn't flinched an inch. "Is that what you desired to hear, Hekate?"

Hekate remained stoic, her two beings stepping from beside her.

"Search every inch of the Underworld. I want no stone unturned." She said to them, each side splitting off in either direction.

"Please do. I have nothing to hide."

Hades resisted a fanged grin, watching Hekate head straight, striding past him to another corridor.

They wouldn't find her lest he wished for her to be found.

Chapter Thirteen
DESPERATE SEARCH

*I*t took days for them to search the entirety of the Underworld. All its parts, even the most horrific of them. Determination fueled them as they scaled every crack and crevice, unwilling to accept that Hades had no partaking in her disappearance.

Hades sipped thick crimson from the skull of an unfortunate soul, quirking the corners of his mouth.

As far as they knew anyway.

Hekate was obsessed with finding incriminating evidence against him, she and Demeter having a rather close bond. The witch's prowess was becoming involved in matters that did not concern her. Her heart was always in the right place. Her nose, however, was not. Although she had a section in the Underworld, her dabbling in necromancy banishing her here, still she pretended to have no involvement in his company.

The storming footsteps of the sorceress neared, Hades licking red from his fangs.

"Find anything?"

Hermes excused himself from Hekate, bowing before the two.

"I need to return to Olympus, I will return soon." His golden irises locked to Hades, and if Hades wasn't mistaken there was a glisten of betrayal. Hermes couldn't hold his gaze for long, snatching it to the ground. The blond rose, the heels of his winged gilt sandals fluttering. He vanished in a ball of light, the slits of Hades' serpent pupils thinning to nonexistence.

Hades lost the taunting jeer, his grim countenance mirroring Hekate as she stood afore him.

She lifted her hand, a wilting, blush flower petal between her fingers.

"I know she is here, Hades. I will find her." Hekate murmured, Hades masking his worry for the goddess. A wilting petal was certainly not a good sign, his memory reeling all those years ago when she was drowning in a lake. She had been so pale then, succumbing to death. As entertaining as she was to have around, he didn't wish her to be a lost soul, forced to remain here.

"What makes you so sure? Any of Neráida's faeries could have left that behind. Their world is connected here, and you know how fond Neráida is of nature." Speaking of those useless pests, weren't they supposed to be watching Persephone? Why would she be in any danger?

"I don't think faeries would care to be wandering through an endless labyrinth. A punishment so cruel to an inhabitant of the Underworld, to wander endlessly in a panic. Monsters chasing them around for all eternity. That doesn't sound appealing to a faerie. Maybe a curious young Goddess who is unaware of the terrors that lie within."

Reckless girl. This would be the second time she would beseech him in death.

Hades clutched his fist.

"Don't you have a pitiful girl to find? Why do you waste time here?"

Hekate wore a victorious simper, her other two forms splitting from her.

"You're right. Demeter must be waiting anxiously for me."

SEVEN POMEGRANATE SEEDS

Cerberus, who had been pretending to slumber at the foot of his throne, peeked open an eye, the three sets of ears perking in alarm. Hades rested his feet on two heads, the creature unenthusiastic about being used as a footstool, stifled from lunging at an advancing visitor.

"Mother." A yawning stretch came from a young sorceress entering his lair. Her awry midnight ringlets crept from beneath the fabric of her cloak, the silk material sliding back along her thick mane to fully expose the mussed tresses. Rubbing a fist to her iridescent eye, she continued forth, moving directly passed Hades without so much as a glance.

The disrespectful imp would be none other than Circe. Uninvolved in most of the affairs of Olympus, she occasionally ventured here to visit her mother, though their interactions were scarce. Circe was one to isolate herself from any affairs, something Hades admired about her. He wished her mother was the same.

"Circe, you show now that my search here is complete? I summoned you three days prior."

"I was asleep."

"For three days?"

"Yes, mother. Being a sorceress is awfully tiring. Men came to my island, and I turned them all into boars." Her hysterical cackles brought her to crumple and grasp her stomach. "How laughable it all was to see them running about on their hoofs, squealing in confusion. Next time they will be more respectful when they put their filthy shoes on my soil."

Hekate pinched the bridge of her nose, heavily exhaling.

Circe moved past her mother, to a man hanging over the mirroring surface of the soul filled creek leading from the entrance.

"I'm in awe, what a handsome man." Circe purred, Hades rolling his indigo irises over to where Circe was captivated. She had circled around a blond man, reaching carelessly towards him. She cupped his unenthusiastic mien, his dulled orbs lighting up upon catching a glimpse of himself in her crystal-like irises. "May I have him?"

Narcissus was the man's name; a soul Hades hadn't paid much attention to. Nothing but a spoiled cretin, he simply punished the conceited boy by taking away his reflection, which proved to be an effective punishment. He was utterly miserable, unable to see the one whom he loved most. Himself.

Hades waved his hand, shooing the two away.

"Please. I have no use for him. Take him as a parting gift." Circe ripped Narcissus from his punishment, her craft easily disposing of it. Narcissus kept his sight locked to hers, Circe stroking his sharp jaw. His lapis gaze once again held life, Circe amused by his enthralled reaction. Her nails threaded through his short blond tufts, gradually trailing over his toned being.

"Let's go, you shall live with me now." Circe and her claim dispersed in a smoky cloud, her mother soon to follow.

"I'm certain our paths will cross again, Hades." Hekate tossed the petal to his feet, the delicate creation swaying to the crumbling stone floor. When Hades snatched his attention back to Hekate, she was gone.

Hades wasted no time, leaping from his throne and snatching the petal along the way.

He gritted his jaw tightly, watching the petal darken as time ticked by.

Hades had to quickly find his flower.

The human world was no longer its lively green, colors diminished into shades of brown, sickly yellow, and gray. Dying plant life went uncared for, farmers losing their crops in mass amounts, their cattle succumbing to illness, starvation becoming an epidemic. It was ugly, Hekate finding that this was almost as tragic as the Underworld.

Since the disappearance of her daughter, Demeter has

neglected the land she once flourished. All were doomed to suffer if Persephone was not found soon.

Demeter took slow steps beside Hekate, and Circe. Hekate wore a dingy cloak to shield her appearance, as did the other two goddesses to blend in amongst the meager human life.

"I'm sure she simply ran away. Women her age are known to do that," Hekate glanced over to Circe, her child tugging along Narcissus in their search. What she would use the selfish man for was beyond her concern, and Hekate had long accepted she could no longer intrude on Circe's doings. "They're quite mischievous at this age, I should know."

Before them, Hekate's other two forms appeared, Hekate spreading herself out to cover more ground. Her counterparts; one belonging to the Underworld, the other Olympus, held a torch each. Their unwavering expression of stoicism offered no consolation.

They found nothing.

Hekate sighed, turning to Demeter.

"Where was it you last saw your beloved, Persephone?" They had been wandering the roads for hours, searching high and low without lead.

Hekate briefly recalled the flower petal and clutched her fist. If Persephone was in the Underworld, she had to be sure. She couldn't accuse anyone if she did not have solid proof she was there. She couldn't give this grieving mother false hope.

"In the forest. She had been helping me bloom wildflowers that were late to blossom." Demeter's emotionless regard disheartened Hekate, the poor thing all cried out, having such little hope for the safe return of her delicate daughter.

"Why the upset now? It is your fault she is gone." Circe spoke unsympathetically, clinging to the arm of her newest pet. "If you hadn't been so overbearing, she might not have left." Circe hinted to her mother, her iridescent irises lingering over Hekate. Hekate ignored her daughter's hints, Demeter stopping the search party in their tracks.

"My daughter was taken from me. I saw it." Demeter defended against the hotheaded sorceress. Circe shrugged her shoulders as she continued to berate the Goddess of Harvest.

"Many see what they want to when they are guilty. It was certainly an illusion."

"Circe, quiet yourself." Hekate reprimanded, folding her arms over her chest. An agitated exhale exhausted heavily from her lips. "Alright, it is obvious that we are not finding anything useful going in circles with one another. Let's go our separate ways, at dawn, we will return to Olympus-"

"I'm not allowed to step foot on Olympus for Zeus and his pigheaded party think low of me. Courtesy of your unskilled craft, mother." Circe bowed mockingly to Hekate. Facing Demeter, her calloused speech offered not an ounce of remorse. "And truthfully, I have no interest in finding this goddess. She can rot in soil and help the flowers grow that way if need be."

Demeter had been reduced to sobs hearing Circe speak of her daughter's plausible outcome, and Circe had remained completely and utterly apathetic. The way her lip curled showed her disgust at the sniveling Goddess.

Hekate knew that her daughter would prove to be stubborn, yet still, she hoped that her daughter had carried some good in her heart. That she would have some sense of sympathy for a young Goddess such as Persephone.

"Circe, please. We carry similar powers, and it will be easier to find her if we all search together."

Circe chuckled, grabbing the face of Narcissus who had been silently uncomfortable the entire time.

"Did you hear that? My mother is pleading for my assistance." Circe then cast her cold glare to Hekate. "To help the same Gods who cast her out of Olympus." Hekate gave up trying to convince her black-hearted daughter to commit kindness, instead turning to her readied bargaining chip.

"If you assist, I will speak to Zeus about allowing you onto

Olympus." Circe stifled her laughter, her countenance awestruck having heard Hekate's offer.

Circe hadn't a chance to reply when Demeter's hoarse growl intruded.

"No. I will not allow such a dreadful abomination to step foot on our ground."

Having heard the foul insult spit at her, Circe came to her final decision, stalking in the direction of the wooded forestry off the road.

"All well, I see my help is unneeded. I wouldn't wish to be amongst such a perverse bunch anyway. Your husband is filth, I'm sure his eyes linger on your daughter too, wishing to fill her with his seed." She gave a flick of her wrist, a cloud of black miasma consuming her and Narcissus. "Find that child on your own, I hope her eyes are consumed by maggots when you find her."

Hekate looked to a swollen-eyed Demeter, moving to comfort her.

"Demeter. Now was not the time to protect your pride." Hekate drew her gaze from the empty space where Circe had vanished. "Come now, it is growing dark. We will continue this search on our own."

❦

Dreary and utterly exhausted, Demeter slumped against a hearty oak tree, its forage matching that of the rising sun. Its glowing reflection rippled over the still lake, a shade of gold washing over Demeter's tanned complexion. Her aching soles had endured walking to the end of the world and back. So it had felt.

Her dried throat yearned for the crisp, cool water. She knelt at the lake, her white gown becoming sullied with traces of mud. It was pure instinct to drink having not eaten or had much concern for her health for weeks.

She dipped her hand into the crystal surface, small fish swimming frantically upon her disturbance. She took sips, the refreshing drink waking her tired senses. She washed the water over her face soon after, going to dip her hands in once more when her wrist was grasped.

Demeter gave a startled yelp, a presence pushing through the surface. His curled ink locks were drenched, droplets tracing over his muscular frame. His sea-green sights latched to her, Demeter's brows furrowing.

"Demeter, such a picture of beauty. It pains me to see you cry." Poseidon hitched onto land, sitting alongside Demeter. "I have not found your daughter, but I will continue to search endlessly until she is safe at your side once again." This brought her to smile sadly, tucking a loose strand that had fallen from her braided hair behind her ear.

"I appreciate it greatly."

Poseidon leered, his perverse eyes scanning over Demeter.

"You know, young Persephone wouldn't wish for you to be saddened. It's possible she took a little stroll. Women her age are rather adventurous." Demeter shook her head, trying to explain she was certain that Persephone was abducted. It was Poseidon's lips that silenced her, Demeter becoming paled as she brushed him away.

"Poseidon, I cannot. I need to search for my daughter-"

"Why do you turn me away? I can bring you comfort, my dear Demeter." Poseidon held her chin, his mouth lingering as his breathy words cascaded over her skin, her flesh prickling uncomfortably. "I can make you forget for just a while," His touch crawled over her exposed thigh, slowly creeping up her garment.

She slapped his hand away, shooting to her feet.

"I don't need comfort. I need my daughter. She will be the only one who can comfort me." Demeter spat, leaving the frowning God of Sea in the yellowing grass.

She stormed off without so much as a word more to him,

absolutely infuriated. She couldn't believe she was going to allow her daughter to marry him.

She marched through the endless trees along the riverbank, and it was when she heard the snap of twigs behind her she began to speed up. He was following her. Closer the menacing steps grew, Demeter full on running through the woods and towards the open field.

His gravelly voice beckoned her from behind.

"Demeter, why are you running?"

She gave a worried glance over her shoulder, stumbling and scraping her palms as she pushed herself to her feet once more.

It was when she saw a herd of grazing horses in the opening, Demeter hatched an idea. She needed to lose this pesky God, his unrelenting passionate advances not something she desired or had the time for.

Rapidly she transformed herself into a sleek tawny horse, her dark mane coming over one earthly toned eye. She trotted discreetly over to the herd, the creatures accepting her with no issue, having sensed her strong presence. They continued to chew on grass, Demeter doing the same.

She believed herself to be in the clear, her anxious orbs shifting around at those who surrounded. A sigh tickled her lips, however, just as quick as relief came, her cold back held weight, Demeter flickering her gaze over the stunning midnight mare that mounted her.

A terrified whinny followed her wide eyes.

She had not escaped Poseidon after all.

Chapter Fourteen
THE LABYRINTH

"*T*ime is different here," Neráida announced to a sulking Persephone.

The Goddess of Spring was growing tiresome of this place. It reminded her too much of the mortal world, and though she adored the smell of flowers, and the odd wildlife that would flock to her, she yearned to return to him. To further explore the world of which she would rule in her time here.

She had told Neráida that she had been here for too long. She had lost count of the days, and she was growing weary that Hades had abandoned her here. He wouldn't dare, would he?

The thought sparked anger, Persephone shooting up from her place in the grass.

She moped here long enough, she would return whether he wanted her to or not.

None of the faeries were around, and neither was Neráida, Persephone pleading to be left alone. Neráida granted her wish, so long as she remained where she was.

Although she reassured Neráida she had nowhere to go, Persephone was going back on her word. She did have somewhere to go. She had a place in the Underworld, and be it pretend or not, she felt more at home there than she did amongst the bright and beautiful landscape. She yearned for the darkness his sanctum held, hidden from the eyes of all aside from him.

She didn't belong here, growing more restless with each passing day.

Thus, Persephone ventured off into the thick forestry, the setting sunlight painting the passing trees hues of reds, and beige. Quite beautiful, but all the same to Persephone who was eager to witness the lifeless world Lord Hades had to offer.

During her travel, her gaze instantly focused on a fissure etched in a stone wall ahead. It appeared deep, summoning Persephone towards it.

She hadn't taken notice that the surrounding wildlife had become greatly scarce, the tittering of Neráida's faeries silent. A gust of wind traveled through her curls, splaying the dark tresses over her bemused moue. The sun had even dimmed, clouds hovering overhead, plant life wilting under the graying sky.

Persephone hitched up her gown; a blush shade, pink roses stitched throughout the skirt of her garment. It was attire fit for a Queen, Neráida insisting she always needed to dress her part. A Queen could not lack in her appearance for her subjects always must acquaint her with beauty.

Nonetheless, this garment was constructing, and awfully heavy.

Persephone gripped the ruffles of her skirt, grunting as she traveled uphill.

She was beginning to believe Neráida gave her such heavy garments to keep her chained here.

Persephone finally grew close enough to inspect the crack in the mountainous rock, finding that it was wide enough for her to squeeze through. Her touch skimmed over the rigid surface, another breeze swaying her hair.

The intrigued Goddess could not resist the urge drawing her forth, Persephone pressing her back against the lip of the opening.

Holding her dress close, she shimmied, her fingers feeling along the narrow walls as she strayed further away from the light. She soon became enclosed in darkness, unable to see what was behind her or in front of her.

She dared not go back, figuring if she made it this far, she might as well continue.

A strange energy surged through her, Persephone tripping forward.

Her feet stumbled over cracked stone, Persephone's bewildered orbs taking in the tall walls. Dead vine entangled in the ancient rock, stains splattering her surroundings. She couldn't make out the disfigured splotches very well, having been adjusted to sunlight, they failed to see in darkness.

Persephone tilted her head heavenward, shades of swirling crimson replacing the vibrant blue sky. Eerie as it may have been, she breathed out in awe. She had never seen such a color overhead. Blues, oranges, pinks, peach. Never had she seen the deep crimson. It harbored the same color her wound had when she first pricked her finger on a rose thorn.

Taking a step forward, a splash startled her. Persephone staggered back into the wall.

The same wall she had crept through, only the entry had vanished.

Persephone spun around, feeling around the wall, certain this was where she had entered. She hadn't even moved much, she couldn't have gone anywhere. Persephone looked down at her foot, the warm substance beginning to dry on her skin. The bottom of her dress carried traces of cerise, as did her sandals. A low growl was heard behind her, Persephone slowly turning her head over her shoulder.

From afar, the shadowed creature huffed, a cloud of dust lifting from the floor when it flared its nostrils. She could not make it out clearly, but from her standing, the creature was certainly not friendly, and lacked any sort of attributes. It was muscular, carrying deathly horns on its large head.

SEVEN POMEGRANATE SEEDS

Persephone rapidly flickered her eyes to the fresh red puddle, then around at the other patches staining elsewhere, a torn limb was visible in her peripheral. The sight should have nauseated her, however, her gaze sprung elsewhere.

A scream was heard somewhere in this chamber, beyond the towering walls, sending a shiver down her spine.

The monster afore her scratched its hooves, preparing to charge at her.

Persephone snapped from her befuddled haze, deciding now was better than any to start running.

She hitched up her dress, racing down a narrow path.

Where had she wandered off to this time? Her mother warned her that her curiosity was not a safe trait for her to have, and now her mother's nagging was filling her thoughts.

Her palms pressed against a dead end, Persephone hearing the creature gallop not too far behind.

Rapidly, she whipped her dress and rushed down another stony path. Bones lay rotting away in the grime of the floor, dead vine entwining in the eyes of empty skulls. Another cry was heard overhead, her heart hastening as she began to pant. Her hair had lost its neat state, becoming a mess of untamed curls in her dash.

Cutting in front of her another creature stalked, bird-like wings spanning from its back, gangly claws stretching from its fingers and toes while the entirety of the being was covered in feathers. Its beak opened, the loud screech emitting from it piercing her ears. She covered them, the ringing muting the whimper that shed from her lips.

She could feel the vibrations of the bulky monster behind her, Persephone snatching her wild gaze to a broken rock at her side. She snatched it up, hurling it at the bird-like creature in front of her. Its sharp beak opened in a startled cry, Persephone rushing past once it flew off to the side.

Her legs were beginning to tire, the goddess' knees giving out. She scraped her leg on the filthy floor below, trying desperately to regain her footing. Her lungs were on fire, her fingers clutching her chest that violently ached, forbidding her to breathe. It seemed that no matter which direction she went, all led right back to where she began. Where was the end of this maze?

The horned creature caught up to her, Persephone spinning around.

She couldn't run anymore.

Either she would meet her demise here, or she would fight for her life, and she certainly wouldn't succumb to him. She wouldn't be weak; a Queen was never weak.

Persephone watched the beast race towards her, glaring it down. It had skidded to a halt, giving Persephone time to react. Persephone lifted an opened palm, cracking her hand across its snout when it had abruptly lost the power it held. The beast appeared frightened, the ferocious flames dancing in her cinnamon orbs certainly frightening it off. Persephone gave a victorious smirk; though, it was not little Persephone the beast was terrified of. The grimace in her stare was nothing compared to the deathly azure eyes that lingered over her shoulder.

The creature cowered away, vanishing into the shadows.

A rough hand spun her around, and it was then she understood why she had graciously grazed the lips of death.

It was because he was standing right behind her.

Still, she was the least bit enthralled to see his presence. In fact, her hands folded into fists at the sight of him. He didn't seem happy to see her either, his mouth curled into a sheer.

"Stupid girl!" He clutched her face to examine the light scrapes she earned while in this endless labyrinth. The indigo flames licking his skin flaunted his anger, Persephone's creased brows matching his wrath. "I told you to remain with the faeries, did I not? I told you to wait for me-"

"You abandoned me! Did you forget me?"

The silence between them was as heavy as the stench of rotting flesh lingering amongst the walls.

SEVEN POMEGRANATE SEEDS

Hades dropped his hand, a pink petal falling from his fingers. He shut his eyes, his soft cackling the least bit kindred.

"You're childish." Hades gripped her wrist, losing all amusement in his features. "Let's go. You've caused enough trouble." Persephone snatched from him, Hades astonished by her rapid movement of reeling him in by the collar of his shirt.

"You will not be forcing me to go anywhere. I came here willingly, and that is how I will continue to travel. I am not your prisoner. Are we clear, Hades?"

Locked in her raging glare, he couldn't help but compare her steaming stare to that of the crimson sky above. So red, lacking the softness of earthy brown. In her moment of lividity, he was absolutely captivated by this sinister beauty that had been stifled beneath the saccharine surface of warm daylight, and lively nature.

"As you wish, flower." His toothy grin reduced the stern glance he provoked, Persephone relaxing her rigid hold on him.

Persephone set him free, petting the wrinkles from his garment that she had caused.

"I'm still cross with you."

"Blame your lengthy stay on Hekate. She insisted on searching every foot of the Underworld for you."

Persephone refused to spare him a glance, Hades bowing his head in efforts to redeem her innocent sights.

Hekate, a rather talented sorceress, was not one to be undermined or easily defeated. Persephone was irate she had gotten involved too. She supposed the search had reached a desperation only she could console.

"I will blame none other than you." She whispered. "If you desire my forgiveness, you will need to earn such a privilege."

"Wasn't saving your hide enough? They would have devoured you had it not been for my arrival." It was then she shared with him an unsettling smile.

"I would have loved to see them try."

With that measly phrase, his affections for her had grown,

the taunting dare of death to consume her quite alluring. She knew he would never allow such gruesome events to occur. Or it was possible she truly believed she could defy his presence, invincible to the mortal afflictions of demise.

Hades held a hand out to her, Persephone placing her dainty touch to his blackened fingertips.

Blue flames raced along her arms, enveloping her in a steady warmth. Hades' azure glance drew off to the side, finding an array of black roses had bloomed, lining the dried, thorny vines. Beautiful creations certainly caused by her excitement.

He drew her close, the ash of the crackling fire beginning to transport them from this eternal torment, unfit for the Goddess.

"Will showing you the entirety of Underworld earn your forgiveness?"

Persephone's sparkled in enthrallment, her prior irritation fleeting.

"Even the most gruesome?"

"Whatever you desire." Hades dipped his head, his mouth leveled to her ear as he drew her close to his chest. "It is only natural that a Queen grows familiar with her territory."

The final ashes of their beings were swept away, sent off to another section of his Kingdom.

※

As they strolled through various places of the Underworld, Hades explained she had crossed a portal, one unintentionally left open. *"You've just witnessed one of the many punishments. A never-ending labyrinth. One of no escape or rest. Eternal fear."*

Side by side, they leisurely strolled through the remainder of the Field of Punishments. She watched the tortured souls pushing a large rock uphill, only for it to roll down, forever stuck in an endless loop of pushing this heavy stone uphill. She witnessed a soul sitting in shallow water, a fruit tree dangling above their head while they hopelessly reached for the sweet that would forever move from their grasp whenever they dared to yearn for it. The roaring growls of hungry demons chasing their victims, screams of those enduring boiling oil, being burned at the stake, and even having vultures feed on their conscious bodies struck no fear into Persephone.

Hades explained each of the foul acts in detail, Persephone taking the tour in rapt silence as they traveled forth.

Adjacent to the punishments had been the Field of Asphodel, a sanctuary for ordinary souls. Miles of merry, mortal beings were racing through the tall grass, drinking nectar beneath towering fruit trees. The children were all curious by her presence, approaching the Goddess carelessly despite Hades at her side. A few even padded over to him and offered him minuscule insects they had caught. He knelt to their level with a tenderness she had seen him lack, a sincere beam given as he ruffled their hair.

The dead seemed to appreciate him here, none harboring any crude feelings towards him, though it would be unwise if they did for he was the one who cared for them. False sunlight felt so warm against her skin, and for a moment's time, she could have been fooled into believing she had returned to the mortal world.

They had left all too soon, Hades pointing out to her Hekate's portion, a path leading through thickets of dead trees, a measly wooden shack spared for her.

"Truthfully, I was even hesitant to give her a place considering the disgust she expressed towards me... and the fact she was returning the dead to the living. Unfortunately, it is here that the outcasts of Olympus linger." Persephone held his arm, she and Hades treading to the end of the dirt path. A pier and a large body of water separated them from an island, Persephone hearing all about it was a child.

Elysium. An island where banished Gods and Goddesses came to live in bliss for all eternity.

"And just over there, Elysium." Hades murmured. He didn't seem too pleased to speak of it. "I rarely tend to anything on that island, they can take care of themselves." Persephone saw the discomfort discussing the ungrateful beings living amongst him. Hades could have chosen to allow them to live eternity in a void, yet he had provided his kin with a place to continue their celebratory antics of guzzling wine, and laughter.

Hades recoiled from her hold, the whip of his cape snapping as he faced away.

"I apologize for cutting your excursion short, but I've suddenly grown tired."

Persephone noticed the change in his tone, clearly annoyed by Elysium. How hurtful they had been to him in their lives and surely, they were cruel to him even now. Entitled and uncaring even living under his protection.

She faced from the island, following in his stead.

"There are hundreds of acres to explore, as I swore it would take days to seek every inch. Once you learn the pathways here, you are free to explore to your heart's content."

Persephone latched onto him once more, her cheek resting against his shoulder.

He silently accepted her affection, stiff, yet unwilling to cast her away.

If Persephone could live at his side for all eternity, she wouldn't have any quarrels on the matter.

Chapter Fifteen
POMEGRANATE SEEDS

The Goddess of Spring returned to Hades' sanctum, overseeing all the Underworld from his obsidian balcony. She had undressed from her blood-soaked dress, exchanging her floral appearance for the subtle black of her shadow gown, stitched for her when she arrived.

The twinkling lights of fire over the kingdom sparkled in Persephone's cinnamon irises. The eerie architecture held its own definition of beauty, the miles of darkness lit in soft shades of black, blues, reds, oranges, and yellows.

Hades was rested on his bed, his attentions admiring Persephone a great deal. The wind shifted her long curls, swaying her dress in its gentle caress.

"This might be my favorite place in all the Underworld." She looked over her shoulder, pieces of her luscious locks that were the color of healthy soil fanning against her soft, sun-kissed skin.

Hades rapidly flickered his slits elsewhere, wandering over the silk tapestry above.

"Because my bed resides here?"

Persephone stalked over, her giggling hastening his frigid heart while she playfully swatted his arm.

"Certainly not, don't flatter yourself." She teased, her eyes venturing back to oversee the Underworld. "I don't think I could ever grow tired of it. Have you?"

"It doesn't excite me much. I've been forced to gaze at it for hundreds of years." He despondently retorted, his scrutiny dilating when they drank in the innocent appearance of Persephone. His claws dug into the silk sheets to stifle his desire to caress her. "I'd much rather gaze at you."

Persephone blinked at him, confusion parting her lips. His sudden admittance of admiration stunned her, having never had a man say such things. Unsure how to accept what he had said; her cheeks became a twinge of pink while her boisterous laughter filled his chambers.

"Oh? What was that?" Persephone mocked once the air returned to her lungs. She expected him to shyly brush the comment under the rug, however, her teasing provoked him, Hades gripping her cheeks.

"I said, I'd prefer to admire you."

Persephone raised her brows, speaking through her puckered lips.

"Are you confessing your affections for me, Lord Hades?"

"A man can appreciate beauty and have no amorous feelings." Hades eased his touch, his charcoal thumb brushing over her plush lips, silky as a rose petal. "Alas, I am not just a man."

Persephone snickered, snatching from his touch. Surely, he was just toying with her, the God of the Dead couldn't feel the warmth of love, could he?

"Is this one of your tactics, gain my love to further irritate my father-"

"I am sincerely intrigued by you, Persephone." His earnest tone was one the pair was unfamiliar with, Hades himself unable to recall such tenderness in his words. "I look forward to what other mischief you will cause."

It was then he snapped from the spell she had put him under, Hades shaking his head. Why was he babbling nonsense? What had brought these odd feelings about? Had it been her defiance? No, it hadn't been just her defiance alone. Something in him dragged her down here to the Underworld, and while it may have started as a harmless gesture to provoke the Gods, he found himself enjoying her company. While she had been away in the realm of faeries, he found himself itching for her return, irritated that Hekate was taking up his time. They had been apart far too long, and he hadn't realized how empty it felt without her here.

He had never shared a bed with someone who was warm as sunlight. Only once they rested together, and while she had fallen asleep with ease, he could only stay awake and savor the heat she emitted. Sunlight he loathed for hundreds of years was embodied within her. He yearned for her to return. When Hekate had shown him the petal, he panicked and would have turned over his Kingdom to find her. He would never admit that, but he would've done anything. He couldn't live with the thought of being alone any longer.

"Speaking of mischief, I have a certain faerie Queen to reprimand." Hades climbed from bed, Persephone grasping his sleeve to prevent him from abruptly leaving.

"You cannot just express your feelings for me and leave."

Hades gently took the hand that stopped him, pressing her knuckles to his lips.

"Yes, I can. I'm a God. I can do whatever I wish."

"And I'm a Goddess. My say is equally important."

"Is that so? You are in my Kingdom."

"Our kingdom." She corrected.

Hades snickered, placing his hands on either side of her.

"Ah, yes our Kingdom." He pulled her close, his smirk hovering over her grinning lips. "That tongue of yours will be your downfall here." Persephone creased her brows, as he leaned towards her parted lips, no longer smug. His whisper caressed her prickled flesh, a soft gasp given. "Let's discuss the matter of yours and mine over dinner."

As quickly as the utterance tickled her awaiting lips, she was whisked to a long dining table. She rapidly flickered her gaze at her still spinning surroundings, skimming over the hematite crystal chandelier overhead. The black marble table afore her was layered with plentiful food, plates stretching across its length from her, to where Hades sat.

He was slouched in his tall chair, his wardrobe had completely changed, though just a moment ago they had been a hair apart in his bed. Strands of his raven hair cut over his deep azure irises from beneath the crown of bones he wore, embezzled with sapphire gems. The collar of his ebony tunic was undone, exposing his ghostly complexion in contrast, his sharp collar bones matching that of his carved features. His fangs were buried in a turkey leg, ripping the meat off the bone violently.

"Help yourself." He pointed the leg over the choices of food.

Persephone caught her reflection in a silver chalice, finding her appearance altered as well. She matched the interior of the gloomy dining area, a breathtaking dress that resembled cooled embers, glittering with rubies that sparkled when they caught hints of light. Her lips were stained the color of wine that ringed their glasses, her brunette curls drawn up into an elegant updo.

She had finally grounded herself, figuring Hades used one of his little tricks to conjure them as they were.

"Queen Neráida says that once I consume anything from the Underworld, I will be damned to stay here for all eternity." She recited, her fingers curling into fists beneath the table.

He gave a questioning quirk of his brow. "So you don't wish for that, flower?"

"Do you?" Her expression was hurt, her eyes twinkling. "I understand that this arrangement was merely mutual for us to commit to our yearnings; for you to be vengeful towards my father, and for me to explore a world other than that of sunlight-

" Persephone's voice was as scalding as the flames that existed within him. "But you're teasing a little too much, aren't you? I've made it clear that I am captivated by you. Do not mock me." She sneered, shoving back the chair.

"I don't know what else to say to convince you I am being sincere. What reason would I have to be dishonest? Do you believe me to be the despicable creature your relatives speak of?"

"Why should I believe you share my adoration? How do I know you are not jesting in your words?"

Hades materialized at her side, grasping her rosy cheeks. He dipped his head, unexpectedly snatching her into a kiss. All the air had been drained from her lungs, reminding her of the night he had whisked her off her feet and brought her here to the Underworld. How enthralled she had been. How roughly her blood pumped in her veins. Her chest squeezed, Persephone recalling her second meeting with the Lord of the Dead. Drowning while awaiting his arrival.

Her fingers curled and bunched the fabric of his tunic, her eyes wide.

Never had a man bestowed his lips upon her, her mother chasing off any man who dared try to appeal to her before coming of age. Shock washed through her in waves. It rose the little hairs on her nape, her face flushing significantly. The heat that swallowed her up was as scorching as the flames he had inflicted on her once. This time, he was not being malicious. He tended to her with the utmost care and having his lips caress hers was euphoric. Her knees reflexively grew weak, Persephone's eyes becoming hooded as she supported her weight against him.

His tongue invaded her mouth, its slick texture inviting another sensation. Lumpy. Sweet. Her teeth bit into the buds of saccharine coating, a burst of tartness spilled over her taste buds. Hades withdrew from their affection, still cupping her face, as his voice became a soft hiss against her swelled lips.

JASMINE GARCIA

"Seven Pomegranate Seeds for every year we have been apart. Swallow them, and you will remain at my side for all eternity, Persephone."

And without a moment's hesitation, she swallowed.

Chapter Sixteen
IMPISH BRIDE

That night, Persephone had earned her title.
Persephone. Queen of the Underworld.

"Now," A wicked grin splayed across his features, clasping her wrist. "I believe someone is intruding on our special occasion, isn't that right, Demokritos?" His viperous gaze flickered to the back of Persephone, the tap of hooves bringing her to peer over her shoulder. It was Hades' goat companion who she had been introduced to upon entering the Underworld. He had looked at her with distaste, and that expression had yet to waver.

"Hermes is returning. He is trudging through the tunnels now."

"Hermes. I knew he was to return. He too must be suspicious of me." Hades whisked Persephone off her feet, Persephone clutching him, her head still spinning in her decision to consume the forbidden fruit. "Come, my bride. Time to put on a play for him, aye?"

Her silence was her consent, Hades snatching his false conquest to a stony piece of land just past his sanctum, small spouts of grass pushing up rock, and a once dead tree budding red flowers. It would have seemed since her presence here, life was growing in places that were dark and dreary.

Hades tossed Persephone from his grasp, rapidly pinning her wrists over her head before her knees hit the ground. Her eyes were wide as she was held against the tree, twine tying around her wrists. The roots clutched her ankles, holding her prisoner.

Green snakes weaved through the binding, hissing as they wound around her arms. Her heart thumped with excitement, her eyes sparkling as she watched Hades bind her up. His taunting jeer had vanished from his countenance, his concentrated breaths heated against her flushed flesh.

"Does tying me up excite you, Lord Hades?" Hades snapped from his focused doings, a chuckle leaving his chest. His hand wound around her throat, Persephone's hooded eyes filled with lust, as she nibbled her lower lip.

"At least try to be innocent, flower." Thorns broke her skin, droplets of red racing down her arms. She gasped, Hades tightening his hold, a little smile perking the corners of her mouth.

His other hand guided over her gown, burning away the fabric. Ashes swept away with the chilling breeze fanned from the nearby river, and as he burned away her dress, a spider descended from the branches above. Persephone crossed her eyes, watching the brown spider crawl over her chest, its white silk began to spin over her. Rapidly the strands began to weave a garment, covering her chest and creating short, loose sleeves. The rest of the dress stopped above her knees, the wavy fabric silky against her tanned skin.

Persephone watched the carob bodied critter retreat to the leaves and couldn't hide a smile.

Arachne.

"Hermes, you cannot just barge into Lord Hades Sanctum-"

"Try to stop me, Demokritos, it will not end well for you."

Hades heard their voices booming through his Sanctum, Hades loosening his hand from around the Goddess' throat. "Behave yourself now." He murmured, his azure irises lurking off to the side, where Hermes exited his Sanctum, all four of them united.

Demokritos bowed, Hades stroking his talons over Persephone's bruised neck.

"Hermes."

Persephone remained motionless beneath his touch, limp with only entwining branches to hold her up. "You came recently, hadn't you? Why return so early?"

Hermes was horrified momentarily, his mouth agape as his eyes ventured over Hades' maiden.

"Dear Gods, why have you taken her?"

"Oh, my bride?" Hades bunched a handful of her dark locks in his fist, ripping her head to the side so her displeasured mien faced Hermes. She cried out, shutting her eyes. Tears pricked her squeezed lids, wetting her long lashes. "Because she smelled delicious." Hades buried his face in her neck, Persephone flinching at his abrupt actions. He inhaled deeply, his raspy utterance breathed against her rough pulse. "I wanted to see if she tasted as sweet." He gripped one of her bound wrists and squeezed. Thorns buried themselves deeper into her, a gush of crimson spilling along her arm. Hades brought up his head, Persephone following his motions to rest her head on her shoulder. She watched his forked tongue glide along her tender flesh to lap the blood. She tugged the restraint, more warmth flooding over her tied appendage. Heat flowered in her belly when their eyes met briefly, unable to conceal a moan.

"She does. Like nectar." He flashed his red-stained fangs at Hermes, the Messenger seeming to become stoic to Hades. His touch scaled from her wrist down her body, Hades shifting so that he was adjacent to Persephone.

"I wonder if her innocence would taste as sweet," Hades began gliding his touch along the contour of her curves, his fingers bunching the skirt of her dress. "But I won't know until I undress her." He breathed heavily into her ear, the friction of her thighs doing very little to stifle her yearning. She bit into her lower lip, anticipating his touch to venture further. She truly hadn't cared at that moment whose eyes were on her. All that she craved were the indigo gaze that lingered over her.

"Do you think me a fool?"

"What do you mean?"

Hermes huffed, pointing to Persephone.

"Her thighs are quaking. She obviously enjoys you. Please save such displays for your chambers."

Hades dropped his hands, giving Persephone the gift to catch her breath. She drank in the air to her quivering lungs, her hot skin growing cool when she had been abandoned.

"And what conclusion are you drawing? Any virgin squirms under the touch of a man, desired or not-"

"Hades."

Knowing Hades could not best the intelligent Messenger, he laughed as he slacked his shoulders. He then rolled his attention back to her.

"Persephone, naughty nymph." He tsked, pacing back to her. He tilted up her face, Persephone blushing fiercely. "You certainly are no good at pretending, my flower." Hades waved his hand, Persephone stumbling forward into his grasp.

"If she were truly afraid, all this life would be wilted. They appear to be thriving to me." Persephone flickered her eyes over to the budding tree, whose flowers had now bloomed, a beautifully sinful shade of red. She snatched her eyes to Hermes, the Messenger approaching the two. "Persephone, do you understand the great deal of pain you are causing in the mortal world?"

Persephone turned her cheek, residing to Hades' chest.

Realizing his accusations would not get the young Goddess to respond, he turned to Hades.

"Why? To anger Zeus?"

"You read me so well. Am I truly that predictable?"

"To me, yes. I've come to you for years, since your banishment."

"I kidnapped Persephone originally to simply anger her caretakers," Hades moved aside her hair, exposing her soft features.

"However, I have come to adore her. As you can see, the situation has become...quite sticky so to speak." Upon closer inspection, Hermes noticed red stained the corner of her mouth, moving closer to brush his thumb over the residue. He tasted the substance, the bitterness widening his eyes.

"You've eaten his fruit? Do you understand what you have done?"

"Clearly. Just like you are no fool, neither am I." Persephone removed herself from Hades' grasp. "I will reign over the Underworld. I am more than a child who raises flowers. I am the burning flames of the sun. I am the deceased that feed the soil. I am the maggots that consume decaying corse. I am life after death. I am Persephone. Goddess of Spring. Queen of the Dead."

Hermes hadn't recognized the once docile damsel, the one who graced floral life and sowed wheat alongside her mother. An innocent maiden, orbs as wide as a doe still unfamiliar with the world. Now all Hermes witnessed were embers in her eyes coming to life in her wrath.

"I ate the deathly fruit willingly. I bit into his seeds and swore my loyalty, and it is here I will remain for all eternity."

Behind her, Hades simpered, placing a hand on her shoulder.

"What will you do, Hermes? You cannot have her. Spare her the grief of returning to a place that stifles her true power. Will you take that away from her?"

"You've tainted her." Hermes jutted his chin, accusing Hades of his wicked play.

"I've done no such thing. Seek the seers who Persephone had pled to in search of me. She sought me. Craved the darkness I had to offer. She was drawn to it. Just like I was beckoned to her blinding light. You cannot take away what fate has bestowed upon us."

Hades leaned over her, Persephone holding her confident stance. Her head was tipped up, glaring at Hermes. The power that exuded from her was beyond that beside her mother.

"Look at how this flower flourishes in the dusk."

Hermes swallowed roughly. His Adam's apple bobbed, a streak of perspiration racing down his temple.

"You know me better than all. I would have never brought harm to an innocent."

Hermes fell to his knee, bowing his head to Persephone.

"Forgive me for thinking you incompetent. My tongue will remain stone in my mouth unless Zeus directs me to speak of your presence."

That is all Persephone could ask of him. Hermes could not go against a command of Zeus, being a messenger between both he and Hades. He did not have the freedom to choose sides.

Persephone stalked forward, picking up Hermes head in her palms. The warmth he was used to had returned to her sweet expression.

"Thank you, Hermes." She placed a kiss on his forehead, the heat of her lips scorching. It was then she moved aside him, leaving his presence at her leisure.

"Goddess of Spring. Understand your absence is causing your mother a great deal of distress." She paused in her steps, her glowing irises gazing over her shoulder.

"I'm sure. But I will not sacrifice my happiness for hers."

She left the men to their conversation, disappearing into Hades Sanctum.

Hermes rose, keeping his gaze cast to the ground. Hades rested a firm hand on Hermes' shoulder.

"Shielding you from the truth was not out of distrust, Hermes. You understand I couldn't tell you in fear of you returning the finding to Zeus."

"I know." Hermes gave a hefty sigh. "If you simply desired to enrage Olympus, you have done so. Her mother is destroying the mortal world, her lack of care given due to the obsession with finding her daughter. Haven't you noticed more souls entering the Underworld?"

"As I've said. I have fallen in love with Persephone."

"I thought you were still playing a part in front of her." He admitted, Hermes cocking a brow at the sneaky God. He had known the God of the Underworld for years. Lying was not a trait of his, therefore Hermes had very little reason to doubt him. Howbeit, love was hard to believe.

"She will not be returning to Olympus, and I couldn't care less of those barbarians."

"Hades, you must understand. The mortals are suffering-"

"Mortals die every day. It is of no concern of mine. There will always be a place for them here." Hades' venomous tone spat, his cape whipping as he stormed from Hermes. "If you tell Zeus about her, I will understand. It is your duty, but you best be certain I will chain her to the depths to keep her here, Hermes."

Upon his display of expressed affection, Hermes slumped in defeat. It was hard to believe Hades inhabited such emotions, yet not surprising. Many desired the hand of Persephone. She was one who awoke amorous feelings amongst men, even the great Aphrodite jealous of Persephone's attributes.

He couldn't bring himself to tear apart the two. They had chosen one another to live for all eternity, both clearly smitten. Hades especially. To show genuine adoration was not something Hades quickly expressed, and now Hermes spotted a difference in his manner. How gloomy, and cynical he had always been. To have such light in his life draw out his sparse compassion meant far more to Hermes than it did to be a trusted messenger. Hades had been punished for far too long.

"I will not mention this, so long as she is safe. But I cannot say for certain I will not be forced to speak of it."

Hades began to stalk away in pursuit of his flower.

"As I've said. Tell Zeus. Scream it to the heavens. Persephone will forever remain here in the Underworld."

Persephone scrubbed her injured skin, plucking thorns from her arms and ankles. Crimson swirled the cool river water, little red orbs coming to her aid. Aíma, healer faeries peppered her wounds, tending to them gently as Persephone failed to. The sting of the punctures faded beneath their care, the gaping holes in her wrists closing.

An Aíma fluttered afore her, its deep garnet curls shades darker than the faded color of her flesh. The shape of their wings was abrasive, and deathly looking, transparent wings with specks of red dust coating them. An absolutely darling creature.

It gave her a bow, before gathering the other faeries, and zipping off.

Persephone examined her purified skin, skimming her fingers over the healed surface.

Oh, how embarrassing.

She could not play the part of a helpless damsel as Hades expected her to.

Persephone dusted herself off, deciding to leave from the edge of the riverbed, and amble to his chambers.

She seated herself in front of the vanity given to her graciously by Neráida, the flowers dulling in color. She plucked a jeweled foot of a raven from the collection of beauty instruments, running the sharp talons through her curls.

What if she had ruined everything Hades had planned?

"Your Highness." The deep voice beckoned from the doorway, Persephone jolting at the unfamiliar tone. She peered at her reflection, a man lowered to his knee catching her attention in the corner of her reflection.

Persephone cleared her throat, adjusting her white dress.
"Yes?"

The man looked up, Persephone taking in his pale olive skin. His ink tufts were askew, a shadow of facial hair adding to his rugged appeal. Drawn into the scruff were swirls, an ancient looking pattern. He lacked a wardrobe, Persephone coming to realize, this was none other than-

"Cerberus. I apologize for the abrupt entry."

Persephone acknowledged him, giving them permission to meet her eyes. They glanced up, slowly rising to their feet. Persephone found herself staring up at a towering man, her back arched to keep their gaze locked.

"Is there something you need? You've caught me at an awful time." She said, turning from them, settling herself on the edge of Hades' silk sheets.

"I only desired to personally meet our Queen. I had yet to truly admire the woman my master shares his throne with. You're quite beautiful."

Persephone smiled, bashful by theie sincerity. They knelt, scrutinizing her shyness.

"But you lack that ferocity I had seen prior towards Hermes-"

Just as quickly her expression became mortified.

"You witnessed that? Aren't you supposed to watch the gates?"

"No need if there isn't a threat entering." When Cerberus noticed her distress, they expressed their regret. "I apologize if you felt I was intruding. I hadn't meant to."

Persephone groaned, laying back in the bed. She couldn't help how Hades made her feel, and all that she had spoken had jumbled from her lips before she could stop.

She closed her eyes momentarily.

She hoped Hades wouldn't hold her behavior against her.

"Cerberus. Please leave. I need to speak to your Queen in lonesome." Hades' firm utterance drove Cerberus to obey, bidding his farewell to Persephone.

Once they were alone, Hades prowled at the foot of the bed, Persephone sitting up in the slightest, raised on her elbows.

The silence was killing Persephone. The maiden was dangling an apology on her tongue when Hades gripped her ankle, and ripped her to him. Her eyes were wide, Hades snickering as he hovered over her parted lips.

"I cannot tease you so and not finish what I have started, aye?"

Her befuddlement earned Hades to mimic her moue.

"You're not angry with me." Hades settled his weight atop of her. He clutched her wrists over her head, a gesture she was keen to be noticed in their prior engagement.

"Why would I be? I have no reason to be cross with you."

"But your plot against Zeus-"

"Will occur regardless of your affections."

"They will find me Hades."

"So let them. You will not be leaving, you've condemned yourself here." The hiss of his breath tickled her pulsing jugular, Persephone still bothered by her obscene actions. She squirmed tugging the hold he had on her, Hades' bruising love bites peppering her exposed neck.

Her nails dug into his shoulder blades, scrunching the fabric of his clothing. Involuntarily, a pleasured exhale wove into her utterance. "And Goddess, my behavior-"

"Was awfully alluring." Hades gave her a toothy grin, his hand traveling along her curves, under the skirt of her dress. Before she could give another ounce of concern, a gasp warmed her cheeks, Persephone flinching against his touch. "Now silence yourself. I don't wish to hear pitiful concern. All will be taken care of." Hades playfully nipped her lip, Persephone succumbing to giggles as his caress grazed along her thighs. "You especially, my flower."

Chapter Seventeen
SECRET GARDEN

The smallest smears of red stained her fingertips, Persephone eyeing her glistening release in the light the faint flames offered. He hadn't truly hurt her, the slight discomfort of their unruly actions only now rearing its ugly head. While their bodies were entwined in ecstasy, she felt nothing of the sort. Just his rigid form, and all its glory.

The burning ache of her body and her flushed skin had long simmered down, leaving behind a tired and worn Persephone. Her chest ached, her unsullied hand clasping over her tender heart, still violently beating.

Hades seized her wrist, his forked tongue tasting her wet touch.

His wicked beam provoked a similar gesture from his flower, Persephone blushing and looking away. She hadn't been with a man prior to him, and to be so exposed; for him to be so exposed, it was a vast change to the fiery brunette.

"You were not so shy before," Hades turned her face to him. "Why so modest now? Hmm?" He teased, reveling in the innocent nature of his beloved. How her silvery tongue seemed to melt against his skin. Having caught her coy mien, she exchanged his banter.

"Was I too filling for you as I predicted? You seemed awfully tentative." She retorted.

"I was merely savoring. I prefer to taste my meal before I consume it."

Hades pressed her into the bed once more, hovering over her. Her fingers guided through his damp hair, gently over his chiseled cheek.

"I think you've had enough, no?" From her hooded gaze and the dwindling embers in her softening irises, her exhaustion was visible to him. As much as he desired her, having not felt so passionately for many years, Hades settled alongside her.

"You can never have too much of something that does not fill you." Persephone enlivened then, glaring at him. "I only jest." He chuckled, Persephone abruptly straddling him. His teasing awoke the lust buried beneath tired bones, the sleep in her eyes vanishing. The subtle blue flames in his chambers flickered to a hue of red.

"I suppose you're right. Something delightful can never truly fulfill you. You'll always crave more once you get a taste."

Hades grinned, his hands traveling up the curve of her waist, and over her breasts. Persephone cupped her touch over one of the hands that tended to her, her thick curls casting over her simpering lips as she tilted back her head. Her gaze was locked to his, her jaw dropping in a gasp as she took him in. A rough thrust tightened his hold on her, Persephone inclining forward.

"And that is why I will remain here forever. I can never leave my King unsatisfied."

***

Sitting in the flower beds, faeries clustered around her. She tended to the thirsty flowers, caring for the unwanted plant life that had grown in his sanctum. The patches of greenery kept his Queen happy, though she claimed she wouldn't have minded if he had gotten rid of them, he knew that as the Goddess of

Spring, she needed the comforts of home if she were to stay here.

He watched from his throne, Cerberus in their womanly form keeping Persephone company.

Although irritated that Persephone had taken their place in his bed, Cerberus saw the impact Persephone had on Hades. The stoic God smiling whenever the blossom was present.

"She's happy." Neráida had stationed herself at his side, uninvited. Hades hadn't spared her a glance, focusing his gelid eyes on Persephone. His stoicism a facade for his subjects, had been broken the moment she looked to him, a vibrant smile so wide it closed her pretty eyes. He couldn't control the quirk of his mouth, and it hadn't gone unnoticed by Neráida. "And she brings an equal amount of light to you."

He said nothing, continuing to watch her play amongst his subjects. They all seemed to enjoy her as their Queen. All but one, who was frowning in the shadows of Hades kingdom. Demokritos.

"Ah, I warned her to stay away from you." Neráida sighed in defeat. "But like a snake, you charmed her. Slithered between her legs and promised something you can never truly give her."

Hades disregarded her statements of her doubt in his affection, his monotonous inquiry responding instead.

"Is it ready yet?"

"Not yet. Soon. My faeries are working diligently."

"How long is soon, Neráida?" He lifted his head from his palm, glaring at the Faerie Queen. "I'm still quite annoyed that she ended up in the labyrinth under your watchful eyes. I am running thin with you."

She laughed, her head falling back.

"You do not strike fear into me, silly God." She breathed out, the rest of her laughter trickling from her quivering lungs. "But I will not rush. I desire this to be a special place for Persephone when she desires to get away from you."

"Oh quiet, imp."

"Hades!"

He had an annoyed choice of words linger on his tongue when he faced his maiden, any of that agitation dissipating. In front of his nose was a flower, his azure eyes crossed to the lavender stalk.

"Doesn't this one smell lovely?"

Hades inhaled, taking in the sweet scent. The faeries giggled at their interaction, none having seen such a soft display. Hades glared in their direction until they dispersed with frightened squeals.

"It does."

Persephone laid the flower aside, climbing onto his lap.

"But I smell much better, don't I?"

Hades remained indifferent, Persephone shifting atop of him. He grasped her nape, rendering her still. He leaned in so only she would hear.

"You taste better too,"

Persephone then burst into laughter. "Surely I do. Most flowers aren't meant to eat, my Lord." Hades couldn't withhold a smile as he grazed his knuckles along her pink cheek.

Queen Neráida looked on, a small but visible smile lifting her lips as she watched them interact.

"Queen Neráida! Queen Neráida!" Little voices screeched, earning the attention of the three, the impatient creatures tugging at the hem of Neráida's leafy gown.

"Yes?"

"It's ready for her highness!"

Queen Neráida looked to Hades, who began to ease Persephone from his lap. She rose to her feet, her gilt sandals slapping against the stone.

"Come with me, my flower. There is something I must show you."

Persephone was befuddled, preparing an inquiry when her hand was snatched. She was guided behind him, her gaze flickering to Neráida who only smiled knowingly.

His steps were long and purposeful, almost excited, Persephone noticed as she half-heartedly stumbled behind him. The walk was a small travel across the river, Hades trudging through the shallow end, and assisting Persephone over the crossing stones.

On the other end, an unfamiliar gate halted her path, one she hadn't seen when Hades had guided her through the Underworld. Perhaps she had missed it? After all, she had yet to truly explore the vast kingdom.

The gate was tall, the bars spread enough to see through, yet she could see nothing. It was awfully dark, as expected here in her new home.

The gate eased open on either side, Hades holding out his hand. "After you."

Persephone eyed him, nevertheless making her way inside the blackened space.

Upon her entry, golden light soared through the trees, lighting the vast scenery.

She was awestruck, pastures of green striking her vision. Trees went on for as far as her eye could see, vast foliage reminding her of the place where she was raised. Her eyes glittered, taking slow strides inside. Miles of flowers colored the land, available in all hues. Both striking and subtle colors cluttered the grounds, the bushes, trees. Her fingers grazed over silky petals of white lilies as she passed, soon prickling over the rough texture of pink floral hedges. Crisp fruit dangled from trees in all directions, in the center of the grove none other than an ancient pomegranate tree, its roots thick with age. The trickle of lake water shushed nearby, the chirping insects hiding within the long grass adding to the serenity.

Her heart swelled, the warmth of home radiating over her tanned skin.

A ridged pedestal cut into her vision, the cream post and swirled flattop holding an intricate piece. Gems sparkled against the false sunlight, catching her attention. Small obsidian and ruby jewels dripped from a crown. Weaved of the darkest roses, skulls of small animals were stitched between the roses. Persephone approached the stand, Hades clasping cold fingers around the headpiece. She looked up to him, Hades gently placing the crown over her unruly curls.

"A place just for you, my Queen."

Tears brimmed in her eyes, her gratitude stuck in her chest when Hades abruptly grasped her wrist, and brought her to the pomegranate tree. He placed her palms on the bark, ants crawling along the wood, avoiding her hands. "This is not all, I would not be so cheap in my gift to you."

Persephone creased her brows. "You're absurd, this is a marvelous gift in itsel-"

"Close your eyes. Change your surroundings." Persephone was confused, looking to him for further explanation. "Go on, eyes closed." He covered her eyes, blocking the marvelous light from Persephone's vision.

Change your surroundings.

The bark beneath her fingertips liquefied, warmth rushing down her arms and pooling at her ankles. The sway of water pushed against her feet, the scent of dewy grass filling her senses.

Hades dropped his hand, allowing Persephone to witness what she had envisioned. Persephone blinked, the warm luminance vanishing, replaced by frigid navy light. Eerie, yet delicate it washed over her setting. The grass had become soft soil, bearing mushrooms that spread onto trees. Most were poisonous, the flowers too carrying deathly qualities. The exotic plant life was vibrant even under the dark rays of the night.

"I called upon Neráida's faeries to bestow magic unto your garden so that you may be anywhere at all."

She peered around stepping through the flowing water of a river she had created.

"I never want you to feel trapped or grow tired of the Underworld. So, to you, I grant a paradise that you may change as you desire."

Her breath was snatched from her lungs by the sheer beauty. Persephone climbed from the ankle-deep riverbed, turning to Hades.

"You had said that looking over the Underworld grew tiresome over hundreds of years. In the years to come, will I stop exciting you?"

"Never. This was a life of hadn't gotten to choose, but you... I've chosen you as my Queen."

"This gift was awfully foolish-"

Hades appeared to deflate, stalking in Persephone's steps as she began to retreat to where she had rooted the pomegranate tree. "I needn't a changing home. I am content with my current home. It is one I can never grow tiresome of, for each day I wake, it is a new day. I can look at the blue skies for hours," She motioned to his azure eyes. "I can be pricked by thorns." She scaled her fingertips over his lengthy nail beds. Dragging her touch back up, she giggled as she wiped her thumb over his lips, exposing his elongated teeth. "A creature can playfully nibble my skin."

She sighed, getting on her toes. "All the comforts of home lie within you." Gently, her rosebud lips pecked his parted ones.

"But I do love the gift." She tittered, Hades still captivated by her touch. "It is beautiful. My own little piece in the Underworld." She whispered, numerous flowers sprouting at her feet, grass tickling their soles. Persephone dragged him down abruptly, Hades' stumbling as the two collapsed into a bed of posies. Their laughter grew soft, Persephone resting a hand over his chest. "Let's stay awhile."

He kissed her forehead, adjusting her crooked crown as he did so.

"As you wish."

"Why are you so kind to me?" Persephone was seated before Queen Neráida, visiting in order to thank her for such a grand gesture. The Faerie Queen smiled as her faeries played amongst Persephone.

"I've known Hades for many years. A companion of the sorts. He helps tend to my world and my creatures, something not many would do considering their common reputation for trouble. You are aware, yes? Faeries are considered manipulative, so they have no place in the mortal world. It is only right I tend to his happiness as well. And you are his happiness, Queen Persephone."

A warmth radiated through her chest remembering Neráida's words from the prior night. She was his happiness. Persephone stalked from her green pastures, closing her gate behind her.

She needed to help rule, she was not merely here to look pretty at his side.

She was here to tend to the Underworld, and Hades had made that clear when he had decorated her with a crown.

Persephone adjusted the beautiful headpiece, swiping the loose grass blades from her shadowed dress. She had gone to Hades, who was settled on his throne. He was watching over the Underworld when she asked him, "What can I do here as Queen?"

"Anything you yearn to, flower." He simply said, offering her a beam.

And so, over time, she would help wherever she could.

She would spend time in the Field of Asphodel, offering her company to small children and animals. She had the duty of consoling a grieving child, who had succumbed to death due to starvation. Persephone's heart hurt for the young girl, Persephone assuring that her family would soon join her. Wiping away her tears, she ushered her to play amongst the other children.

Persephone had also spent her days assisting Hermes in guiding souls into the Underworld to Demokritos, a goat man who appeared to have loathed her. She, however, paid him no mind. Hermes' brilliant personality would always outshine the dreary task, the two talking as they guided souls, brought comfort to them along the way. Seeing how blissful the Goddess was, he never spoke of the horrors above, keeping her ignorant to the ordeal.

Persephone giggled as their conversation ended, stopping at the end of the pathway to leave the souls with Demokritos.

"Alright, precious Goddess. Until we meet again." He mockingly bowed, Persephone shooing him away.

"You always do this, please go back already. I have no time for your teasing, Hermes." Their laughter had finally snapped Demokritos, the stomp of his hoofs startling them as he approached.

"This is a place of death, how dare you disrespect it so." Demokritos was quaking, his nostrils flaring like an angry bull.

Persephone raised a brow, sidestepping the cretin. "Hermes, have I told you about my garden? Hades had it made for me, and it is absolutely stunning." Hermes snatched his eyes from the creature, moving in pursuit of Persephone.

"I suppose I can spare time to visit." The two walked in linked arms, giggling amongst one another while Demokritos stormed behind the pair. He continued his lecturing.

"You do not belong here, Goddess of Spring. You need to go back to where you belong!"

Continuing to ignore him, Hermes was impressed by the variety of plant life coloring Persephone's garden, complimenting her new home.

"Hermes, if you do not tell Zeus about the Goddess of Spring, then I will." Demokritos warned, both Persephone and Hermes snatching their glare to the goat.

There was a heavy silence, the garden growing dark under the strain of her grimace. Hermes had gone to reprimand the disrespectful oaf when Persephone's stony voice stilled all in her path.

"You dare to speak the name of your Queen in a threat?" Persephone's warm demeanor had been swept with the chilling breeze that shook the trees. "You dare defy me?"

"You are no Queen of mine." Demokritos spat. "You will stop this game to anger the Gods. You are killing others don't you see? They are all starved! Your mother grieves and prevents vegetation from growing. You are destroying the Underworld and everything Hades has created. This a place of death and you desecrate it with your light!"

Demokritos turned his hoof. "Zeus will learn of your presence here, and you will return to your mother-"

It had all happened so fast.

Persephone was stunned in place momentarily, her quivering fist curled around a bloodied blade, her arm extended to her side. A geyser of crimson shot from the gaping hole where Demokritos head used to be, his horned skull rolled off his shoulders, his body slumping into the dirt to feed her flowers. Hades stood in the gateway, an unreadable expression locked to Persephone. Blood sprayed over her sun-kissed face, her gaze glistening as she dropped the blade she had snatched from Hermes belt. The moment of fear forced her hand, that anxious impulse becoming rage. She snatched the lolling head, gripping the black hairs between her shaking fingers. She moved past Hades, into the heart of the Underworld, the entry of the gates bustling with souls and creatures alike.

"Let this be a lesson to you all!" She roared, all stopping and gazing upon the horrific scene of their Queen dangling a bloodied head, red matching the shade her irises seemed to glow in her rage.

Two infernos.

Her subjects shrank at the sight of the seemingly harmless goddess. "Never become my enemy, lest you wish to be at the receiving end of my wrath."

She tossed the head to the stone at her feet, the clunk of his horns resonating the silence.

The whip of her dress fanned out behind her as she fled from astonished eyes.

SEVEN POMEGRANATE SEEDS

She marched towards her garden, slipping past Hermes and Hades, slamming the gates closed behind her.

She breathed out a hiccuped breath, her blurred vision latching to the beheaded body of Demokritos. She killed him. How could she have been so heartless?

He threatened to speak to Zeus. If Zeus knew, she would be forced to leave. Taken from him.

Her sight flickered to the pomegranate tree.

But she's eaten his fruit, could they truly take her away?

The creak of the gate opening spun Persephone, Hades striding in.

"Hades." Persephone pitifully croaked, outstretching her arms. He cradled her tightly, his lips pressing roughly to her temple. "He was to tell Zeus of me, I couldn't let him." Persephone sniveled, Hades shushing her.

"No crying. He was a treacherous miscreant. If you hadn't slaughtered him, I would have." He gently stroked her askew tendrils, eyeing the corpse in his peripheral, the stench of death coating the withered grass. Persephone was still shaking in his grasp, Hades guiding her to the grass beneath the pomegranate tree. "You did well, my flower. They all respect you as their ruler, and I promise you, you've struck such fear, no one else will speak of this." Hades waved his hand towards the body, ribbons of thorny vine shooting from beneath the ground and entwining the corpse. The barbed creation swallowed the body under the dirt, disappearing from their sights.

Still, she remained soundless in his hold, picking the drying crimson on her arms.

Somewhere in her troubled state, she succumbed to sleep, her shift in glum emotion darkening her garden. Hades abandoned his duties for a short period, comforting his Queen.

"Your Highness." A soft voice woke her, the slits of Persephone's half-opened eyes greeted by white-blond strands shifting in the whisper of a breeze. She curled deeper into Hades side, side-eyeing the man afore her. They were knelt, wearing garments that were a size too big for them. It was then she noticed this young man was wearing Hades' dark clothing. She blinked her eyes in confusion, the blond taking hold of her hand. "Never will you have to raise your blade against a blasphemer. I will guard you and fight in your stead. Never will you have to stain your hands again."

Alas, the third and final persona of Cerberus appeared, Hades mentioning that he was a rare sight, never one to interact with many, if at all.

Cerberus took her hand, bringing her bloodied knuckles to their lips.

"You swear my protection?" Persephone murmured, her voice cold and unforgiving.

"My life is yours."

Hades gave a sigh, guiding Persephone from his lap.

"That was more than I've heard you speak since you have been living in the Underworld," Hades said to the monotonous blond. He climbed to his feet, waving Cerberus over. "Care for my beloved in my absence. There is something I need to tend to."

Given the command, Cerberus knelt, taking the responsibility to comfort the Goddess. Persephone resided in Cerberus' side, a new bond of trust between him and his trusted guard of the gates.

Hades barged from her garden, Queen Neráida, Arachne, and Medusa were waiting, all wearing expressions of worry.

"Let us prepare for our next traitor, yes?"

A falling flower petal, and the face of Hekate crossed his mind, Hermes reminding Hades shortly after the demise of Demokritos that she had yet to return to the Underworld.

It would not be long before Persephone was found.

Chapter Eighteen
COLD GODS

*I*t had become so cold.

Ice covered fields, not an ounce of green for miles, for all life had long died beneath blankets of white. Softly, silently, frozen flakes fell from the graying sky in the mortal world. While the sight of frost scaling over the land might have been beautiful, the aftermath was anything but.

Beyond the intricate icicles dangling from barren trees, and frost coating thinly over glass windows, starvation befell the mortal world. Bodies of men and animals alike lay blue under layers of the snow, the cold halting the growth of crops. No wheat meant cattle succumbing to death first, mortals soon to follow unable to replenish their food sources.

Many sat quaking in front of orange flames, their sickly thin appearances of sunken cheeks and eye sockets promised they would soon follow the path to the Underworld.

But she cared not about the withering state of the mortal world.

Demeter caressed the large lump that was her belly, two fetuses stirring in her womb. She was seated before Zeus, the other Olympians at her sides.

"Demeter, Goddess of Harvest. You have been called upon

Olympus today for your hand in the mortal world...or lack thereof."

Demeter kept her empty gaze at Zeus' feet, unable to find the strength to gaze up. She was so weak. So overwhelmed with sadness. The anger towards Poseidon's actions long extinguished under the harshness of the cold weather. She felt empty. Like the trees bearing no fruit, nor budding flowers. Her appearance went unkempt, months passing since the vanishing of her daughter.

Over time, those who had once helped her in her search had retreated. Zeus called off the search, exclaiming they could not look for her forever.

For them to have no compassion towards their own was not an astonishment to Demeter. The Gods were cold, and uncaring for anyone other than themselves.

Although all eyes were on her, she felt one stare in particular wash over her. Her gaze flickered over to her left, beyond Hekate who sat supportively at her side. She met sea-green eyes, his coy attention returning to his mighty brother when she caught him staring. Since he impregnated her, the two hadn't shared a word. This was no secret to any in Olympus. All of them knew she carried his children, but it mattered not. Still, Demeter held her regard to him, sparking the anger she believed to have buried in the mounds of gelid snow.

The grip on Demeter's hand grew tight, Demeter looking to a seemingly unfazed Hekate.

Hekate was clearly uncomfortable in the presence of those who cast her out, nevertheless, Hekate claimed to withhold precious information on her daughter. It was their last attempt at finding her.

Persephone is all that mattered to her currently. Not Poseidon's ravenous behavior towards her, not the dying mortals.

"Demeter, why have you abandoned your worshipers? They call to you, starved, and on the brink of death-"

"Not another fruit will grow until she is found. I will not tend to anything until my daughter is safe at my side once again."

Her quaking tone unrelenting to his final decision. She wouldn't give up in her search like they had. She wouldn't abandon Persephone.

Zeus heavily exhaled, resting a tender hand on her thinning shoulder. "Demeter. We've already discussed this. We cannot waste any more time on, Persephone."

"She is your daughter!" The Goddess screamed, leaping from her chair. "She is our daughter. How can you treat her so?" When he didn't respond, Demeter brushed his hand away, wiping hot tears from her flushed cheeks.

"So be it. I still stand by my word. Not a blade of grass nor a grain of wheat will flourish." Just as Demeter was prepared to leave, Hekate rose, and intervened. She couldn't bear to see anyone suffer at the hands of the Gods, and she certainly couldn't stand to watch this grieving mother. She has been through enough.

"While in the Underworld, I encountered flower petals. Associated with the youthful, Goddess of Spring."

Hushed murmurs began to fill the room.

"And when did you make this discovery?"

"Months before. I was not sure if it was proper to present this with little proof, but it has become dire for me to admit this. A last resort if you will. It cannot hurt to search there once more."

Demeter had been pacified then, shock overtaking her expression of distraught. Could Hades truly have kidnapped her daughter? What for?

Thoughts of Poseidon ravishing her haunted her, probing her silly question.

Why else? A young girl snatched away? What other purpose would she have to him?

All awaited Zeus' commands, finally with a ferocity that his white eyes had lacked before, a bolt of thunder struck.

"If she truly lies in the land of the dead, we will retrieve her."

Hekate looked to Demeter, a glimmer of hope filling the eyes of the pregnant goddess.

"I will send Hermes to the Underworld. He will be my eyes."

Hermes' shoulders appeared to stiffen in trepidation, Hekate taking notice of his odd behavior. Does he know something?

With a whisk of his hand, Zeus commanded Hermes to venture to the Underworld.

※

By nightfall, Hermes had prepared for the dreadful trip he had taken many times before, only this time he would betray Hades. The thought turned his stomach. Hermes approached a portal to the Underworld, the black hole unnerving him in this very moment.

"Hermes!" Down the gilt hall, Demeter hobbled towards him. He waited for the ailing Goddess to approach.

"Yes, Demeter? What is it?" Once she caught her breath, she straightened, clinging to his shoulder.

"If my daughter is truly down there, please, give her message." She brought her chapped lips to his ear, whispering a message that Hermes would deliver. A tear dripped along his shoulder blade, his heart panging for the grieving mother. The Goddess of Harvest pulled away, Hermes stroking the loose strands of earthy hair from her face.

"I will speak your words to her if she is found."

Demeter gave him a pitiful smile, backing away to allow Hermes to trek into the portal down through the passage to the Underworld. The moans and groans of souls reverberated through the tunnel, Hermes keeping a steady pace.

The hike felt shorter than usual, most likely due to his desire to prolong the news of Hekate's suspicion. Hermes approached the gates, the three-headed canine becoming guarded upon his arrival.

"Hermes, Messenger of the Gods. We cannot let you pass."

Their guttural bark warned. Hermes slumped his shoulders, a little grin working its way to his lips, as scratched the back of his neck.

"Cerberus, you cannot keep me out. I am part of this world as well. You are only preventing the inevitable."

Cerberus exposed rows of teeth that could tear through his flesh at a whim, a drooling snarl, bringing Hermes to return to his stoic mien.

"I come with a message for your Queen."

Cerberus too knew they could not stop him from entering, and reluctantly they stalked aside keeping a close eye on Hermes as he strode in. Into the sanctum he went, Hades throne in eyesight.

Hades sat tall and proud beneath Persephone, the Goddess glaring down at Hermes as if he were a mere bug. Her stare was harsh, as scalding as the flames within the tortured ring of the Underworld. From when they had last spoken, after her murder, her gentle demeanor appeared to have vanished. Hades drew his fingers along the slit in her dress, running up her upper thigh.

Three women stood guard at the foot of the throne. Medusa, Neráida, and Arachne.

"I am shocked to see you off your throne, Neráida." Hermes smiled, Neráida not sharing the amusement. It appeared they knew his reason for being here.

"A true Queen will step down and fend for her comrades if needed."

Medusa approached him carelessly, grasping his face so their eyes would meet. Hermes cast his eyes away, her wicked laughter ringing in his ears.

"What a handsome God, won't you look at me?"

When he failed to do so, Medusa set him loose.

"You are an enemy, Hermes." Hades was resting his face in his palm, looking over Hermes. "You are not welcome here."

"I see that." Hermes muttered, adjusting the shoulder of his toga. "I am here to tell you-"

"That Zeus has forced you to return here and find Persephone? We've known long before your arrival." Hermes shut his mouth, his brow raised. "You are the set of eyes in the Underworld? Well, I have eight on Olympus." He motioned to Arachne, the half-spider maiden shifting to a minuscule spider that crawled into the palm of Hades. Persephone took the spider, holding her gently as they resumed their conversation.

"Now with the formalities out of the way, you may return and tell Zeus he can come down and try fruitlessly to retrieve Persephone. But he will not have her."

"Hades, many will get hurt if you force their smite. They are gods, and a meager group of women-"

The four women glared at him, Hermes clearing his throat to rephrase his insult.

"A small group of you had no chance against Zeus and his powers."

"A meager group of women, and a sorceress, Hermes." A seductive utterance purred against his nape, two cold hands clasping his shoulders. Hermes nearly jumped out of his skin, a cloaked woman taking hold of him. She tittered, vanishing and reappearing from the shadows in which she was hidden. A black curl cut over her glowing iridescent irises. He could not clearly see her grinning expression hidden in the shadow of her hood, but he knew it was there.

"Circe."

"Aye."

"You're involved?" Hermes seethed, glaring at Hades. "For what price?"

"The blood of the Queen. A small price to pay for my service." Circe removed an empty vial from her sleeve, holding it out to Persephone. "You will be needing this soon." Persephone took the empty vial between her fingers, and Hermes gripped her wrist in a panic.

"She will curse you!" Hermes spat, his lip curling in disgust. "You will sink as low as to seek her help? She is selfish. Manipulative. She will change your words, she is nothing like her mother."

Persephone snatched her wrist from him, tucking the vial away while Hades snickered.

"I am glad to hear that. Her mother is a useless witch. Circe, however, will serve as I tell her. You have misjudged her."

Circe's grin widened, keeping her attention locked to Hermes.

"Now spit out what you need to and leave. We cannot speak so casually."

Hermes straightened, snatching his eyes to Persephone.

"I have a message from your mother, Demeter, Goddess of Harvest and Fertility."

Persephone looked away from him, leaning her head on the shoulder of Hades. Hermes went on to recite what Demeter had spoken to him.

"Persephone, dearest child. How I've mourned your disappearance. The nights are cold without you, and as time passed, the frigid nights stretched into the days. I miss you dearly, and I am ever so sorry to have allowed you to be snatched away. The horrors you have been exposed to must have been hard to bear, and I swear to those who have hurt you, I will shower wrath upon them. Once you are returned to me, we will live happily, I promise that to you. You and your newest brother and sister that Poseidon had forced upon me during my search for you. Don't shed tears, we will come for you, my darling child, that I swear to you."

Persephone sat up her nostrils flared, angry tears streaking her red cheeks.

"That monster hurt my mother?"

"You've caused her a great deal of pain as well, Persephone."

"I did no such thing!" A crackle of thunder sounded off in the distance. "She deserved the grief she felt. She controlled every aspect of my life. I was to never change with her. I was to be an innocent doe married off to the same monster that forced himself on her." Persephone relaxed her tense state when Hades kissed her cheek. "And most importantly she bedded with a coward of a God. I am forced to share his blood. I will forever resent her for that, and all they have done. They cast out Hades wrongfully-

"Not wrongfully. He was absurd. He didn't tell you what he's done-"

"He committed wrong because he was cheated by the same God you defend!"

"Oh, you're making the innocent Goddess angry." Circe appeared adoring of Persephone, gnawing her lower lip. "Maybe I was wrong to wish her dead. She is quite the Goddess."

Hermes lowered his voice and gave one last plea to the Goddess. He didn't wish to see either harmed. He didn't want bloodshed to come out of this petty dispute. "Just surrender, Persephone. Go back. Be with your mother. Before anyone else gets hurt." He hinted towards the murder Persephone commited. "Before you get hurt-"

"I will not!"

"Hush now," Hades silenced a quivering Persephone, stifling her high-pitched argument by bringing her to rest against him. "Hermes, you've completed your task. Return to Zeus and tell him all you wish. You've chosen your side. I hold no quarrels with you, but I suggest you bite your tongue before you create a lasting enemy." The slits in his eyes narrowed, Hermes knowing he was pushing his luck here.

Neráida then stepped forward, staring down the messenger.

"She will not be harmed. You on the other hand," She swiped her hand, a gust of wind causing him to stumble, and collide with a web engraved in the stone flooring. His sandals became stuck, rendering him incapacitated. Aíma fairies sliced at his ankles, Hermes trying to pull away. Circe stood behind him, tearing him from the trap, and flinging him, and his bloodied ankles out of the gates. "Watch your step."

The gates slammed closed, Hermes left stunned. He dusted himself off, stepping away from a growling Cerberus.

He turned his heel, brows furrowed as he marched back to Olympus.

There was nothing that could be done. It was a fight long waiting to happen between Hades and Zeus.

Hermes clenched his fist.

It turned far more complicated than it should have been, involving a young Goddess, and a mother who played no part in their feud.

Hermes stepped back through the portal, and back into the marble foyer where all awaited his return. A bead of sweat trickled along his temple, Hermes gluing his eyes to the ground as he gritted his teeth.

"Persephone is in the Underworld."

Amongst the crowd, Demeter sunk to her knees, her eyes rolling back while the others attempted to hold her steady.

Zeus was enraged, commanding his soldiers to Underworld, other Gods and Goddesses scurrying about upon his given orders.

Hermes knew the damage was already done. All he could do was prepare for the outcome of this disaster.

Chapter Nineteen
CROSSFIRE

Persephone hugged her knees to her chest, her eyes swelled. Hades was at her side, sitting on the ledge of the bank while Persephone soaked in the teal water, vapors rising to aid the puffiness of her crying eyes.

"I don't want to leave. I want to stay here."

"Persephone, my flower. No more tears, everything will be fine." Hades pleaded, rolling the slits of his eyes to the ceiling. He couldn't stand to watch her cry. It hurt what was left of his heart. The piece that felt affection for her.

The faeries did not speak in excited jumbles, remaining quiet as they spilled water over her back to bathe her. Persephone sank deeper, burying her face in the nook of her arms.

"I killed a man to keep my secret. Was it all for nothing? Was this all for nothing, Hades?"

"No. You killed a creature for me. You devoted yourself to me. To the Underworld and your subjects. Only if I mean nothing to you will you have done it all in vain."

Persephone peeked her pink gaze at him, softly sniffling.

"You mean everything to me. But what am I to you, but a quivering Goddess? Weak and feeble. Afraid when faced with trouble-"

"Nonsense." Hades climbed into the pool alongside her, his clothing becoming drenched and sticking to him. "You've nearly ended your life just to meet me. I would say that is no coward's task." He then smiled, tipping up her chin. "And you've fooled in the labyrinth like a lunatic." Persephone then giggled, Hades wiping his thumb over her cheek. "Cowardly is not a word to describe you. All rulers have their moment of weakness. It is alright to be fearful." He drew Persephone close, settling himself against the rigid bottom of the water, filled with polished rocks and minerals. "What's done is done. Do not doubt the decisions you have made. All were for a reason."

Persephone rubbed her itching eyes, taking in a shaky breath. "Wherever you go, I will follow. That I promise you, Persephone. I will never leave your side, nor will you leave mine. You've already sworn your eternity to me."

"Am I selfish? For abandoning my mother?"

"We are all a little selfish, flower. Nothing to be ashamed of."

Persephone traced the wet fabric of his cape, Hades nuzzling the crown of her head.

"Don't fret anymore. All will be cared for." He drew up her attention, brushing back the wet tendrils that clung to her rosy cheeks. "You will be cared for." He reminded her again, the trickle of water releasing the remaining tension in her body. "Please rest now. Regain your composure." Persephone breathed out, listening to the fairies whispers as she slipped into slumber.

❧

An eternity seemed to pass.

Persephone hadn't slept well since the night of Hermes visit, paranoia eating away at her nerves. Still, she committed to her duties as Queen to the best of her abilities. She nourished the life that lived under her rule. The abnormal creatures and night flowers were tended to, Persephone visiting the souls of children, taking on Hermes and Demokritos duty since neither were present.

All was quiet, Persephone idly sitting amongst Neráida's faeries, and playing a game with Arachne. The spider maiden wove her fingers meticulously through a strand of her web, crossing the pieces over her fingers until the single strand was interwoven throughout all her fingers. She held the webbed shape to Persephone, who would try and gently pluck the strands in an attempt to create the shape along her own fingers, however, the web would collapse, and they would fall into a fit of laughter.

The blond persona of Cerberus rested his head on Persephone's lap, somewhat awake as he laid amongst the flowers, listening to their hundredth fit of laughter in their repetitive game.

Circe was propped on a stone pillar, the violet barrier of her magic disfiguring the exterior beyond the gates.

A loud grunt from Circe broke the monotony, all scrutiny turned to her.

"Where are they?" Circe barked, her hood falling back when she snapped her neck towards Hades.

Hades was calmly outstretched on his throne, taking leisure sips of crimson liquid from his chalice.

"Preparing I suppose. They do fear me, after all. Or possibly, Hermes decided not to speak." He murmured, pursing his lips and swishing his drink around.

"I don't have time to waste here. My magic is not infinite." Perspiration glistened her chiseled features, her dark lips curled into a snarl.

"You have as much time as I need you to have here. We have a deal, Circe."

The witch hissed unpleasant words under her breath, all returning to their tedious tasks.

Neráida and Medusa leaned against the stone walls, appearing on the verge of sleep.

While all seemed eager to have the Gods of Olympus come to retrieve her, she certainly wasn't. Persephone wouldn't mind if all stayed as it were. Quiet, peaceful.

But this was the Underworld, not a place of peace. It was one of unrest.

She watched all her companions fidget.

Just then a thundering boom shot Persephone to her feet, Cerberus shifting into their enormous canine form and nearly crashing into the ceiling.

Persephone stumbled back when Neráida clasped her shoulders, guiding Persephone behind her.

"Remember what we discussed. That barrier will not hold back whatever Zeus has sent. Flee to your garden and hide deep within it." Another quaking thud trembled the ground at her feet, Persephone shaking her head.

"But-"

Queen Neráida snatched Persephone's hand, folding her fingers around a crystal blade.

"Go."

Persephone knew she would only get in the way if she tried to aid them; so quickly, she turned her heel and sped off towards her garden. She cast the quickest glance to Hades, who rose from his throne, meeting her cinnamon irises briefly as well.

The patter of her feet racing through the Underworld never wavered, even after an explosive crackle created a violent wind. Her hair whipped into her eyes, Persephone crossing the shallow river to her garden gate.

She clutched the iron bars, glancing behind her at the shadows stretched in the halls. Blood sprayed the walls, men crying out in horror.

Persephone shoved open the passage to her garden, disappearing in the light within.

Hades strode down from his throne, listening to the rumble of men rushing towards the gates to the Underworld. A spear was thrown, the rain of weapons following as men in armor raced forth and tried to penetrate the barrier.

Circe took a firm stance, holding her hands out in front of her, keeping the barrier steady. It rippled with every strike, Circe's breathing becoming heavy under the strain. Blood trickled from her nose, Circe baring her teeth when the weight of their strength cracked the barrier.

"Hurry," Circe growled to Neráida.

The shatter of her barrier collapsed Circe, the soldiers pouring in. Circe dissipated into a cloud of miasma, the soldiers peering around for the wicked sorceress.

As they stood in confusion, strands of Arachne's sticky web rained over them. They became encased in an inescapable tomb, hundreds of man-eating spiders scattering the floors and feasting on them.

Cerberus charged at those who escaped her trap. Their rabid teeth snared soldiers, tearing their limbs and bodies apart in a bloodied mess. Innards flew, soldiers rushing past the beast that mauled their brothers. The three-headed beast devoured all it could, leaving the rest to the Faerie Queen.

Neráida was at his side, and upon raising her hand, shards of reflective surfaces broke through the ground.

The soldiers of Zeus mumbled in confusion, their backs pressed against one another as they awaited their threat.

Medusa stood amidst the fragments, her form reflected around the group of soldiers. Her head tilted back, a grin curling her features while her wild eyes, as well as the eyes of her snakes became a blinding topaz. She speared her gaze straight through the soldiers, the unexpected men caught in a silent scream as their body turned to stone. A few managed to keep their eyes closed, maneuvering forth the mirrors while Medusa stalked them until they reached Hades, and... Persephone?

Hades looked at his side, witnessing a weeping Persephone.

He looked again, prepared to scold her when he caught a glimpse of green eyes.

Hades was holding a chain that shackled around her wrists, the soldiers racing for the two of them. Hades materialized a flaming weapon, the curved sword clutched in his available grasp, preparing for his battle.

"Stop!" A booming voice halted the men, stopping them short of the unseen webbing of Arcane. A bolt of lightning struck through the crowd, the infamous white-bearded God making a rather shocking appearance. "She is not who she seems."

Hades grinned, dropping the chains.

"It has been quite a while, hasn't it brother?"

Zeus removed his own weapon from his sheath, lightning crackling along the blade.

"Indeed. You have something that belongs to Olympus." The two approached one another, the soldiers sure to keep their distance. "Push forth," Zeus ordered, destroying the layer of unseen webs, the soldiers scattering around Hades.

"Belongs? You speak as if she is an ornament to your collection." The two circled one another. "Though that isn't a surprise, that is your view on others. Everyone is below the almighty." Hades sneered, raising his blade to strike Zeus. Zeus blocked the attack, countering with a sneaky dagger he drew from his belt. Hades disappeared then reappeared a safe distance away. "Reverting to your cheap tricks I see. Pathetic."

The statement seemed to anger the God of Gods and the two charged at one another, their blades clashing, a mess of sparks sprinkling the stone at their feet. Both repeatedly struck their swords at the other, each time the other countering with an equally powerful hit. Neither earned a scratch, an endless dance that Hades knew could go on for all eternity. Both were equal in strength and prowess. It was an endless battle.

A piercing scream faltered Hades, his azure slits casting over his shoulder to the bloodied hall leading to her garden.

"Never turn your back on your opponent." Zeus took advantage and sliced Hades' shoulder, the scorching heat of electricity sliced through him. Hades tensed, his body quaking slightly. Zeus managed another strike across Hades' chest, Hades stumbling backward. The agony blinded him, white electricity sparking from his wounds.

Hades managed to get a grasp on his sword in time to avoid the third clout, Hades pushing Zeus back with a fierce array of slashes, the intensity of his defense getting Zeus to stagger a few steps.

"Help me!" The voice of Persephone echoed through the Underworld, freezing his blood in his veins. The cry ordered him away from a recovering Zeus, Hades vanishing within a forming haze of mist, leaving behind streaks of black liquid. Zeus glanced around in confusion, the fog growing thicker.

An enraged roar could be heard from Zeus as Hades approached the black bars of Persephone's Garden, a bloody handprint curled around the slightly ajar gate.

He hastily burst inside, finding Persephone squirming in the grasp of soldiers trying to calm her. Hades stormed over, clinging to his sword with flames dancing in his eyes. The soldiers saw Hades approaching, a third soldier attempting to attack him from behind, only to befall his blade. Hades stabbed his weapon through the throat of the soldier, slicing upwards and splitting his head in half. The man fell to the dirt, Hades returning to Persephone and proceeding slash at the soldiers. They were mere insects, Hades beheading one laying his filthy hands on her, and the other he pierced his flaming weapon through his heart.

Persephone sighed in relief, her frightened expression vanishing completely.

"Thank you, Lord Hades. But I needn't any assistance-" The voice she carried had become high-pitched and not her own, sounding almost like-

"You're not Persephone." Hades hissed, the faerie shrinking

SEVEN POMEGRANATE SEEDS

down to size and fluttering her slightly broken wing. She dusted herself off, glaring up at Hades.

"Of course not."

Hades then looked around him, soldiers chasing Persephone through forage. On the other side of him, they threw Persephone to the ground and stabbed a sword through her chest. "She is hidden."

He was but a fool falling for his own tricks. This goddess had made him a bumbling idiot. Oh, what she did to him.

Hades stumbled through the chaos, the surroundings changing and growing dark. More trees added to the confusion, the soldiers going in circles as they chased the faeries. Hades tripped, his chest gushing and the trees beginning to spin. He gritted his teeth and had gone to push himself to his feet when a small voice beckoned him.

"Oh Goddess, Hades you're hurt." Her hand was clasped over her mouth, her eyes sparkling in worry. She lowered her dagger that was aimed at him. Her mess of curls hugged her face, her body folded beneath the small space of a large stone.

Hades frowned, his brows creased as he glared upon the girl afore him.

"Are you Persephone?"

"What?"

"Prove to me you're, Persephone." Without hesitation, she poked from her hiding place and pressed her lips fervently to his. Hades eased into her kiss, warmth radiating through his chest. It was Persephone, undoubtedly. She gripped his bloodied collar and snatched him inside. Soft exclamations of displeasure were hushed as they tried to adjust their tangled limbs to no avail. Persephone was squished between his legs, his legs scrunched against the rock wall hiding them. The two were panting, black liquid smearing Persephone's hands.

"What happened to you?" She examined his wounded shoulder. She then looked to the source where most of the blood poured from. She quickly tore at his clothing, exposing his chest.

"Persephone now is not the time for this-" he teased, managing a grin. She shook her head, her expression not as gleeful. Her fingers traced the white scarring surrounding the wound where Zeus made his mark along his chest.

"He's here?"

"As I've predicted."

Persephone bit her cheek, her hands clasped over his injury. Hades was not bothered by the deep wounds, more concerned by the tearful expression of his beloved. He guided her away, blue flames engulfing his hand. He smeared the scorching heat over his chest, the crackling painlessly closing his flesh. He did the same to his shoulder, leaving naught but dry blood and a deep scar.

He listened to the commotion just outside.

It hadn't died down, Hades knowing this would not end until he faced Zeus once more.

Hades beckoned Persephone over, the Spring Goddess easing her weight against his chest. She was curled in his grasp, Hades pressing his lips gently to her head.

"All will be well." He reminded her, burying his face in her thick hair as their bodies began to disintegrate to embers, fleeing from their safety to face Zeus. Persephone clenched her eyes shut, clinging to him tightly.

When the flower opened her eyes, they were seated amongst the comforting bones of his throne, Hades holding her as he often did. She sat atop his lap, sinking into his cradle. She had calmed for the smallest moment when his unsettling voice sent her rigid.

"You know I will not leave here without my daughter." Zeus stood, weapon ready at the foot of Hades throne.

In his rage, blue flames roared over the entirety of him. An immaculate azure that matched his livid scrutiny. The color of ash that masked his thick hair became engulfed in shades of indigo, stretching over his shoulders, and along the length of his arms. Blackened claws clutched his Queen tightly. No one would take her from him.

"She is no longer your daughter. She has already consumed the forbidden fruit here. She is one with this world. She cannot be taken from here."

There was silence, then abrupt cackling echoed the space, Persephone stiffening against Hades.

"That does not matter to me! I could never allow her to be prey to such filth."

"If she truly mattered to you, you would have come long before I've taken her chastity." Hades lifted Persephone's chin. "She is Queen here, the title forced upon her. Like it or not here is where she will remain." A slim blade materialized in his grasp, probing it along her wildly pulsing throat. Persephone didn't move, keeping her solemn gaze locked with his.

"Are you that desperate to keep her? You would kill her and damn her soul here? How laughable."

Zeus approached, Hades forcing the sharp blade to her skin, enough to break through her flesh. He halted his footsteps, Persephone wincing. Hades held firm, his fiery glare burning into Zeus.

"Return to Olympus. I no longer wish to deal with the likes of you."

Zeus frowned, remaining still under the scrutiny of Hades. Locked in a staring match, he hadn't caught the rapid gesture of Zeus' sights flickering off to the side. Hades felt a breath tickle his ear, swiping the dagger to the black form in his peripheral.

In his distraction, Persephone was ripped from his hold. She cried out, Hades catching a glimpse of Hekate. The hood of her cloak flapped, her stoic mien becoming visible to him.

Time slowed.

Persephone's wide gaze twinkled, her dainty hand outstretched to him. Hades lifted a heavy hand, feeling as if he couldn't move fast enough. His arms felt weighted, his claws managing to graze her delicate fingertips.

"Hades!"

Her cape whipped around Persephone, Hades lurching forward from his throne. His fingers wound around thin air while charcoal miasma snatched her away without a trace.

Hades sunk to his knees, dragging his eyes to his empty hands in disbelief. His azure slits scanned the emptiness, when a single flower petal slowly fluttered down, the silk texture kissing his palm.

Leisured footsteps advanced towards the quaking God of Death, a shadow overcasting him. Hades clenched his fist around the petal as he slowly dragged his rancid glare up to Zeus. He confidently stood over Hades, a snarky jeer quirking his mouth.

"You forget. I am the God of Gods. I will always win."

Hades ground his teeth, locking useless insults behind his elongated fangs.

Zeus gripped his chin, bringing Hades' hateful stare to his.

"When will you ever learn?"

Hades snatched from him, Zeus deciding the God had been humiliated enough.

He faced his back to Hades, opening a golden portal for himself.

"Persephone is to never return." He bit, walking through the portal and leaving Hades in his mess of the Underworld.

Bodies were splayed all over the walls, the floor; his sanctum was covered in the blood of faeries, soldiers and his other creatures who had fought at his hand.

All was tranquil, the remaining lives gathering wearily; soft, and saddened by his loss.

"Maybe you should have chained her deep in here as you've said, poor boy." Circe tried to comfort, however, her words felt more mocking than they were pitiful.

Hades slowly rose to his feet, one of his eyes shielded by the strands of his perspired hair.

"Apologies to have wasted all of your time." He said on

behalf of the concerned faces eyeing him in wait. "I will handle the rest on my own."

Hades began stalking past them, muttering to himself. "I will have to be more forceful than I anticipated."

Neráida was first to move, rushing to Hades' side and clinging to his torn cape.

"Now Hades, let's not be haste, you know the trouble you will-"

Hades merely side eyed her, the heated glare alone enough for her to drop her clutch and step from his path. Hades ventured forward, leaving behind his Underworld.

"Cerberus, guard the Underworld in my absence. I will return shortly."

No more playful antics. Hades would turn to brute force to gain back his Queen.

And he would tear Olympus apart if he had to.

He was not to be trifled with, and these pathetic Gods would learn one way or the next.

Chapter Twenty
PRISONER

The Goddess of Spring writhed relentlessly in the hold of Hekate, Hekate setting her loose once they were in the safety of Olympus. Through her blurred vision, the familiar gold and white interior blinded her, quite the contrast from the Underworld. Persephone's steps stuttered forward, unable to regain her footing. Dizziness collapsed her on her rear end, Demeter rushing over to her daughter.

"Oh, Persephone!" Demeter sobbed, crushing a rigid Persephone against her bosom. Even so, Persephone paid very little attention to her grieving mother, so overcome by the lingering fire in her veins as she latched her glare to Hekate.

"What have you done?" The disdain was audible in her quivering utterance, Demeter unraveling her tearful daughter.

Befuddlement creased Hekate's brows, her lips parting as she inhaled to voice her confusion.

"Treacherous witch!" Persephone sobbed, her knees grazing the ground when Hermes took hold of her. He quieted her, swiping her tangled curls from her dirty face.

"Darling child, why do you make such accusations?" Hekate tried to draw Persephone's gaze to hers, but Persephone only shielded her saddened expression against Hermes' shoulder.

SEVEN POMEGRANATE SEEDS

Demeter approached instead, rubbing Persephone's back consolingly.

"Persephone, no need to cry. You are safe now." Persephone allowed the gentle touch of her mother, not for the desire of comfort, but out of guilt. If she hadn't been so rash in her decision to run away, her mother never would have been harmed.

The children in her mother's womb would forever remind Persephone of her selfish ways.

The slap of sandals against marble neared, stopping behind her. A heavy hand promptly rested on her shoulder. Awkward and stiff, she already knew who that hand belonged to.

Slowly she peered from Hermes' shoulder, a sneer curling her lips.

"You." Persephone swiped his hand from her shoulder. "You vile being!" She bit, a drop of saliva flying off her lip, adding to her rabid appearance. "He'll come for me, and when he does. You will be sorry." She hissed, turning to the approaching crowd of her siblings. "You'll all be sorry!"

"Persephone, that's quite enough, surely you are worn from your experience. A long rest is much needed-"

"You be quiet!" She directed Hekate. "I am your Queen. You will not disrespect me any more than you've already have." All knew that Hekate associated herself with the Underworld, so the cryptic words of Persephone silenced all.

"So you did eat his fruit." Persephone became tight-lipped, distancing herself from Hermes. Her spine became erect, her shoulders pushed back with authority as she faced Zeus.

"Yes, she explained how starved she was." Hermes tried to defend. Zeus raised his brow to Persephone, awaiting her confirmation.

"The only starvation I experienced was that of the truth, you power hungry coward."

Unintelligible murmurs filled the space, Zeus holding her challenging stance.

"Pomegranate seeds weren't the only thing you consumed

from him. It seems he had fed you lies as well to soothe that appetite of yours."

Demeter's eyes widened, her mouth agape. "She's eaten in the Underworld? And I was not told of this?" Zeus turned to meet Demeter's frantic eyes shifting from her daughter, to him, then back again.

"I believed him to be bluffing when he had told me." Zeus shrugged unapologetically. "No worries, we will keep her guarded until she returns to her right mind. Once she is rid of his poison, she should be thinking sane once more."

"I am perfectly san-" Strong grasps seized her arms, Persephone stunned by the bruising hold his mindless soldiers took of her.

"Take her. She will be locked away until she remembers that her home is Olympus." Persephone began thrashing, kicking her legs and screaming.

"You will feel his smite! He'll have you all quaking, including you, father." Persephone tugged, and managed to lean herself towards Zeus. "Fear runs on the surface of your face. That is why you banished him. You fear him." The soldiers ripped her back, regaining control over her inconsolable notions.

Demeter rushed over to her daughter, two other guards stopping her. She glanced at Zeus in astonishment, her pleading sights wondering why he was being so cruel. Hasn't Persephone gone through enough? Now to be imprisoned in her own home?

"What is the meaning of this? She cannot be treated like a prisoner, she is your daughter, Zeus!"

"Any daughter of mine would not speak such foul lies to me. When she becomes docile, only then will I see her as such once more. Do you recognize that miscreant?"

Demeter watched as her misbehaving daughter was dragged down the hall, behind a wall.

"She is only frightened, and traumatized. You must understand, he must have hurt her."

"Regardless of the circumstances, I will not be desecrated. As far as I'm concerned, she's a blasphemer." Zeus faced his back to Demeter, the crowd of Gods and Goddesses growing scarce around her now that the scene was over. "Now quit your weeping. Your precious daughter is back."

Demeter was dumbstruck, she, Hekate, and Hermes all staring at one another. Demeter was first to break away, the other two following in pursuit.

"She's eaten his fruit? What is to become of her? Those who consume it cannot ever leave the Underworld. How was she able to leave?" Demeter spoke the fact to those who trailed behind her, eyeing one another with distrust.

"She cannot truly leave. It is only a matter of time before he will come and drag her back down with him." Hermes said to Demeter, removing his hostile stare from Hekate. "Her heart will always desire to return, that is where her soul is bound."

A string of fate; a warning red, ran for an infinite distance, from Persephone, while the other end latched to Hades.

It was a strand unseen by the natural eye, however, a seer would be able to see the unbreakable bond.

Nothing could tear them apart, and though their stomachs turned at the thought, there was nothing any could do, and they were only preventing the inevitable.

※

Persephone was thrown into a gold cage after she was dolled up to Olympus' standards. The handmaids washed her knotted hair from her prior battle, cleaning the scraps and black crust from her hands. Persephone clenched her fists refusing to let them cleanse what was left of Hades. The unclean stain of his blood on her fingers was currently the only consolation away from him.

Nonetheless, she was no match for the four servants, the women prying open her fists with enough force to break her fingers.

A shiny white dress now was elegantly loose around her

curves, the fabric cinched at her waist. Her earthy curls cascaded along her back, framing her pouting face. She clung to the gold bars, a guard at each side. There was nothing in this cell, just a cage for an animal. Or a misbehaving Goddess.

Persephone grit her teeth.

She was not a mere child to punish any longer, Zeus had the nerve-

In amidst her hatred, a disgusting being caught her attention. Sea green irises, and sparkling black hair, a shade of blue beneath the Olympus sun, flashed a smile.

"Ah, Persephone. You've made your mother sick with worry." Poseidon leaned to the bars, Persephone curling her lip in disgust. She hadn't moved, asserting herself to the filth before her.

"Not as sick as you've made me." She spewed venomously. Poseidon smirked at her defiance, hanging his head so their lips were a hair apart.

"Oh, you don't mean that."

Persephone gathered saliva in her mouth, and spat, the slick glob sticking to his chin.

Poseidon shut his eyes, his grin widening as he wiped the mess with the back of his hand. "Feisty, just like your mother." He reached through the bars, roughly gripping her cheeks. Flames danced in her cinnamon irises, her blood boiling beneath her skin.

"Poseidon. I would like to speak with my daughter in lonesome." Demeter set her soft gaze upon him, Persephone snatching herself from his grasp. Poseidon eyed Persephone, slowly making his way towards Demeter. He said nothing to her, brushing past her as if she were a mere servant.

Hermes and Hekate followed, Persephone casting her sights elsewhere.

"Persephone, has he poisoned your innocence?"

The marble beneath Persephone had grown intriguing, anything was other than the worried attention of her mother.

SEVEN POMEGRANATE SEEDS

How ailing her appearance had grown. A wan tan yellowed her flesh, bones visible under the surface of her skin. Her sunken cheeks. Her lifeless hair. All because of her.

Demeter extended her touch, stroking Persephone's sullen face.

"I don't recognize you, yet you have a familiar warmth. One a mother could never forget." A lone tear splattered against the white marble, Persephone leaning into the comforting caress through the cold, golden bars.

"I'm sorry, mother." Persephone cupped her hand over the sickly thin hand of her mother. "It was never my intention to bring you harm. I was just so overcome by rage, I-"

"Speak no more, my child. What occurred was no fault other than Hades-"

"No." Persephone shook her head, her shoulders beginning to shake in her grief. "No, mother, it was not only him at fault. I was to blame. I summoned him. I asked him to take me away."

"Persephone, what are you saying?"

"I wanted him to take me away. You've suffocated me. Sheltered me for far too long. I couldn't bear it. I didn't want the life you have chosen for me. Shielding me from the world, I was to never soothe the craving of curiosity. But with him, I-"

Demeter dropped her touch from Persephone, her brows furrowed in confusion.

"Is that how you've truly felt?" How could her mother be so blind to the overbearing nature of hers? Persephone had been stifled for too long, she needed something more, and that something more was Hades.

"You believe I ate his fruit against my will? I swallowed the seeds willingly."

"Persephone, you must never speak those words to your father-"

"Let all of Olympus hear! He is no father of mine." Persephone exclaimed, her fists tightening around the bars. "How can you still defend him when he's allowed you to mother unwanted children-"

"Persephone, that is enough. Foolish girl. You've allowed your mother to needlessly grieve over your disappearance." Hekate approached, removing the hood of her cloak so that Persephone could witness her stern mien.

"Don't speak to me." Persephone glared the Goddess down, but it was to no avail. Queen of the Underworld or not, Hekate was not to be trifled with. When Persephone lowered her sights, Hekate knelt.

"I had only tried to help you and your mother. I believed you to be in danger. It was not my intention to snatch you away from your happiness. A young maiden does not belong in such a dark place. Darling, you are light. You belong in the warmth of Olympus."

"I left Olympus because I could not stand their pretentious ways! I'd much rather find warmth in flames than in this false light. How they've spun tales on others, stretching the truth. They're just as vile as any within the Underworld." Hekate desperately wanted to convince Persephone that he was the scum of Olympus. That he was no good for a beautiful girl as herself. He was unworthy of her.

"You've brought this on yourself by choosing Hades' side. By being a pawn in his ploy. You cannot blame anyone but yourself. You've befallen to his lies."

"My affection for Hades shall not waver for the only lies I've heard were the ones spread here on Olympus to strike fear of the unknown. To the very end, I will claim myself as Persephone. Goddess of Spring, and Queen of the Dead. None will revoke that title from me no matter where I may be."

Hekate rose from her position, Persephone snatching her grip from the bars, and shifting to the back of the cage.

"If you're against me, so be it."

"Persephone, your mother and I will never be your enemy. Understand, we only want your happiness."

"Then leave me." She stubbornly croaked, facing from them. A silent moment passed before the patter of fleeing footsteps eased her tense muscles, relaxing into her sadness.

"Persephone, he will come for you. Do not fret." Hermes hushed then pursued both her upset mother and an enraged Hekate.

Will he truly come?

In her last moments with him, as her fingertips grazed his own, his panicked eyes locked with her as he tried to seize her.

He would. She had to believe he would.

Persephone hugged herself curling her tired being against the marble floor. She rested her head on the cold surface, a soft breeze racing over her exposed complexion.

Days became nights ticking by unnoticed, Persephone replaying moments of his affection to comfort the painful squeezing in her chest. Persephone clenched her eyes shut, clutching her heart. Her hitched breaths wheezed in the enclosed space, hot tears spilling over the bridge of her nose. Food wilted within the striking sun that poured through the bars, untouched by Persephone. The sun would shift into blue moonlight, and not even the voice of her mother snapped her from her haze. Her lips became dry, cracked refusing drink that was left beside her rotting fruit plate.

"Persephone." Hekate's voice beckoned, Persephone sniffling to stifle her upset. Persephone stirred, her senses returning for a short moment.

"Is it true? You love Hades, Lord of the Dead, God of the Underworld?"

Slowly, Persephone rolled onto her side, her neat hair long undone, sticking to the mess of wetness that coated her face. It glistened against the vibrant moonlight, Persephone blinking her tired eyes. Demeter was at her side, some of the color returning to her tanned skin while Persephone was growing pale.

"I do."

A droplet of water splashed the marble floor.

"He and his subjects have cared for me in my time there. At any moment I could have returned here, and Hades would have allowed me to. I was never imprisoned as I am currently by Zeus." Another droplet pecked the floor, then another.

Demeter bit her lip, turning to Hekate. Her fingers were tightened around something Persephone noticed.

"There is your answer, Demeter. What will you do?"

Reluctantly, Demeter stepped forward, bending over. She held an open palm out to Persephone, a glittering key catching the faint light.

Persephone eagerly crawled forward to her mother, and taking the key between her shaking fingers.

She met the somber eyes of her mother, Persephone's brows furrowing as a light sprinkle of rain began to drizzle down.

"Go to him before he wreaks his havoc," Demeter whispered over a rumble of thunder, permitting downpour upon Olympus.

"Your part is done now. Let's hurry unless you wish to be ill." Hekate whipped her cloak from her body and shielded Demeter.

Persephone clung to the bars, her sparkling attention filled with gratitude as she watched her mother and Hekate flee.

Persephone gripped the key, her fingers feeling for the lock. When she found the opening, Persephone jammed the key in, turned the lock, and threw open the cage.

The guards who were idly standing by for days had woken, attempting to stop their prisoner. Persephone gripped the silver platter on which her food rested, and struck the soldier closest to her straight in the face. They stumbled back, Persephone racing forth into the heavy rain, while the other guard began his chase.

She shoved past shrieking Gods and Goddess running for shelter, making her way to the steps of Olympus.

Faster.

Persephone pushed her feeble legs to run; aching and exhausted she stumbled, slipping on the cream marble flooring. While she tried to regain her footing, the guard clasped her ankle, Persephone glaring at him through her drenched locks. Despite her tugging, he refused to let her go, and so she gritted her teeth, ramming her heel into his knee.

The pain she caused set her loose, Persephone leaving the guard to collect his composure.

She crawled to her feet, splashing puddles in her wake.

The top of the stairs was in her sight. Persephone's breathing hastened, and it felt as if she couldn't get there fast enough. Just a small distance away, he climbed the final step, war engraved in his eerie air. His glowing azure eyes matched the flames that covered him, warding off the heavy rain. The dark expression promised death to all, and so with a relieved sob, she threw herself into his arms. She wept into his chest, clutched to him as if he were her final breath. The sizzling of rain evaporating against his skin had soon hushed, a soft mist spraying from the sky as opposed to the storm.

Hades found his bride, her drenched dress clinging to her body. She looked up to him, her sopping tresses hanging over her relieved mien. Her brows came together, a smiling curling her bluish lips.

"You came back for me."

Hades examined his sickly maiden, noticing how frail she had become in the time they had separated. Though it enraged him, he managed to keep his rage concealed beneath her tender touch.

"I swore I would."

Her fingertips traced up his chest, towards his sharp features, caressing his chiseled jaw until he lowered his mouth to hers. Nothing mattered then, the God of Death at the whim of her affection.

His parted lips brushed over hers, their reunion interrupted by Hermes.

"Hades."

The pair brought their attention to the Messenger, many of their family gathered about and whispering of Hades' return and his affection for the Goddess of Spring. The *innocent* daughter of Demeter.

"Zeus desires your presence. He needs a word with you."

"He will certainly receive more than a word for taking what was rightfully mine." He became tense, Persephone sinking lovingly against him. A gentle gesture to calm his aggression, and it had worked. His fist released, finding its way into her knotted locks.

"There will be none of that, Hades. All we ask is for a civil end." Hera approached from the mass, her delicate heels clicking through the flooded marble. "Now follow. We need to resolve this issue immediately."

Hades glared at the judgmental eyes, forcing them to avert their gaze. He then softened when he looked down to Persephone. He took her slender hand, guiding Persephone proudly at his side. Her head was held high despite the weakness eating her limbs, his presence alone enough to cure how sickly she had become.

He guided Persephone along the slick floors to the council chambers, twelve seats at a lengthy table, six on each side facing the other. They stepped in, shutting the polished oak door behind them. Deep brown, paired amongst white and gold painted the interior, as it did the furniture.

The vast space was decorated with ancient weaponry, locked away in glass cases. It was a warm colored room, yet the air felt so frigid.

Hades sat his love down in a seat, kneeling before her. He drew her face to the side, examining her unhealthy appearance.

"What has he done to you, my flower? Why are you so pale?" Hades dragged his long nails over her exposed collarbones, Persephone shivering in delight. "So thin you've become."

"I haven't eaten. I was too worried."

Hades placed a chaste kiss on her collarbone, his black clutch holding her nape.

"No need to worry any longer. I'm here now." Persephone

stroked his ebony strands of hair, the silky, indigo tinted texture slipping through the crevices of her fingers with ease.

"I've told my mother and Hekate of our schemes."

"It does not matter. I couldn't care less of my retribution towards Zeus. The thought only brought bitter happiness. You give me something far more satisfying. Undying affection. An emptiness that could be filled by none but you."

He rested his head comfortably in the nook of her neck, Persephone's arms winding around him.

"He imprisoned me to keep you away."

"What a buffoon."

"Indeed." She giggled, and upon hearing her laugh he too smiled against her throat. Weakly, she clasped his shoulders, pushing him away. "You should stand. You look like you've missed your conquest. How pitiful." Once he removed himself, she playfully pinched his cheek, Hades taking her teasing hand. His forked tongue flickered past his lips, and over her wrist.

"Oh, but I have. Where else would I bury my-"

The door burst open, Hades slowly rising to his feet as Zeus, Hera, Hermes, and Demeter strode in. Persephone held tightly onto his hand, Hades stroking his thumb over her knuckles to reassure she wouldn't be snatched a second time.

"Hades, God of the Underworld." The four of them seated themselves across from Persephone and Hades, Zeus' white stare filled with revulsion for his brother.

Hades too drew out a chair to sit amongst them, being leisurely in his task.

"Hera. Beautiful as always." Hades grinned, tilting back his head. "Not beautiful enough for Zeus however. You've probably tasted all of Olympus when you kiss your husband-" Hera's cheeks flared red, clearing her throat as she adjusted her peach gown.

"You have kidnapped the daughter of Demeter, Goddess of Harvest, and Zeus, God of Gods. What do you plea?"

Persephone had gone to defend him, to claim she was not

taken against her will when Hades rested a hand on her thigh to quiet her.

"Plea? I plea nothing. I will take my bride back with me. You cannot stop me from doing as I wish. My blood hums through her. Her soul is chained to the Underworld."

"You've stolen what is not yours." Zeus reprimanded, his usual uncaring facade filled with rage.

"As did you, brother. There is nothing more to discuss. I will take with me what is mine, and you all can suffer."

Zeus had lost. Hades reveled in his defeat, the God of Gods believing he had been victorious when he stole Persephone. The truth of his actions stained her tongue. She was never to return to Zeus, and he was imbecilic to believe she could be taken from her new home at his side.

"Hades, you cannot just take her. Demeter grieves for her daughter and cannot tend to the land without her. Without crops, mortals will continue to die."

"And why should that concern me? I have plenty of space in the Underworld for more corpses. I love the company."

"Hades, please." Demeter's shoulders shook, Hermes gently stroking her shoulder while she wept. Tears streaked her rosy cheeks, the sight of the tanned goddess twisting something in his chest. "If you have any good in your heart, you will not take her from me forever. I couldn't bear the thought." Hades lost his jesting smile, his lips thinning into a line. As much as he disliked Demeter, he could not stand to watch her whine, and so he looked to his doe-eyed Queen. Persephone was watching her mother in pity, her sights too glittering with unshed affection.

With that, Hades gave a heavy sigh.

"What will be the compromise?"

"Hades-" Persephone gripped his hand, her wild eyes abruptly latched to him.

"How many seeds has she consumed?" Zeus inquired.

"Seven Seeds."

"Hades, stop it." Persephone pled softly, digging her fingernails into his hand, Hades giving her thigh a squeeze.

"Then it has been decided. She will remain with you for half the year, and the other half she will remain with her mother." Persephone jumped up from her chair, panic sewn into her shaking bones.

"But I-"

Zeus held up his hand, his fierce stare piercing right through Persephone.

"You've brought enough shame upon Olympus. Speak no more."

Hera rolled her blue orbs at Persephone when she followed Zeus. Demeter gathered herself, blotting her pink eyes. Hermes spoke consoling words about Zeus' decision. It was the only fair way to share the beloved Persephone.

"Leave now. You will wait half a year to see her again as your punishment for entering Olympus." Zeus commanded Hades, Hades biting into his tongue to stifle his heated words.

Persephone gasped, stumbling to chase after Zeus, however, Hades caught her wrist, keeping her steady and from causing any more trouble with her family.

Demeter wordlessly trailed behind them, giving her daughter the pleasure of space seeing her seething rage. After all, she knew of Persephone's affections, and she knowingly tore her away from him.

They left Hades to deal with Persephone's inconsolable ire. She stalked away from him, resting her hands on the glossy table. Crystal droplets splattered against the surface, a disheartened Hades attempting to embrace her. He was not prepared for the flames that burst forth. Her balled fists battered his chest, Hades' managing to take hold of her wrists to avoid her senseless swatting. Persephone sunk against him, screaming into his chest.

"How could you agree to that?! How could you? Do you care so little for me?!" He scooped her up, coddling her in hopes she would hush her piercing cries.

"My flower, I love you indefinitely." He murmured into her hair, Persephone taking in shaking breaths. Her fingers bunched his tunic in her palm, unwilling to let go. She lowered her shrill shrieks to match his gentle utterance.

"Then why? Why have you allowed this, why didn't you fight for me?"

"I'm heartless, but not that cold. I can't stand to watch women weep. Especially not one that resembles you." She finally looked him in the eye, Persephone giving him a vacant stare before she shared a little laugh, understanding that her mother's pleas hadn't been ignored by him.

"You're a weak fool."

"Only for you, Persephone." Her parted lips received his kiss, the soft texture of them like flower petals, flourishing against the warmth of his breath. "No more tears now; it will not be long before you come home once again."

Persephone hiccupped, Hades setting her on her feet.

He held out his hand for Persephone, the two making their way from the room, and out into the open where curious eyes awaited.

The mumbles had yet to fade, the hisses of their whispers screaming their names, yet no attention was given. Hades could only focus on the warm skin he would soon depart from.

At the base of the stairwell, he stood.

"Here is where we part, flower." Persephone bit her lip, a poor effort to withhold her sadness. Still, it stained her face. Hades wiped his thumb over her cheek, kissing the tears that had begun to flee. "I will see you soon."

Persephone held his sleeve, nodding her head in acceptance.

"Will you wait for me?"

"For an eternity." Hades took her hand, his lips resting against her knuckles.

Nothing more was said as a dark portal opened behind him, Hades reluctantly grazed his fingertips along her palm, dragging away his touch. His cape fluttered behind him, Hades turning to the portal. Once more he glanced over his shoulder, giving Persephone a fanged smile.

"I will be waiting, my flower."

Just like that he was gone, all too soon for the Spring Goddess. The dreary weather vanished in an instant, the sun bursting through the clouds. Birds came to life once again, enthusiastic chirps filling the air. Despite the scorching sun, she felt utterly cold, her being shivering.

Hekate wrapped her arm around Persephone's shoulders, Hermes too coming to comfort the Goddess.

"Goddess of Spring. Since I am the messenger between worlds, I will gladly assist in your communication with your husband." Persephone softly thanked Hermes, her glum expression finding Demeter waiting not too far from her.

Hekate gave her an encouraging nudge forward, guiding her to Demeter's open arms.

"Come now, your mother has been yearning for your company."

Chapter Twenty-One
TOGETHER AGAIN

The laughter of children playing in the grassy fields caught Demeter's attention from the meadow she tended to not far from them.

Despoina and Arion, Poseidon's children, had been born. Despoina, Goddess of Mysteries, was teetering about, helping her sister pluck flowers from the ground, while her brother Arion galloped alongside them, butting them occasionally with his desire to play. The young fowl circled his sisters, his midnight coat shining against the glare of the sun.

Persephone's brilliant beam fluttered Demeter's heart, Persephone hoisting Despoina off the ground, and peppering her with kisses. Persephone caught sight of her mother watching them, her smile widening as she waved. Desponia turned her head, her curls as dark as the bottom of the sea bobbing when she glanced in Demeter's direction.

The Goddess of Spring pointed to Demeter, adjusting Desponia, so she could see their mother. Persephone grasped her small hand, making the child wave.

At first, Persephone was saddened after leaving the side of her husband, but each night, Hermes came with a message from him. A loving gesture that would remind her of his affection. It wasn't long after when Demeter and Persephone began rebuilding their relationship, that her siblings were born, and she had returned the happy child Demeter had raised.

Demeter gave a long sigh, a brown leaf swaying down from a tree, and landing at her feet. Yellows and reds replaced the vibrant greens that once inhabited the mortal grounds, life beginning to wilt.

It was almost time for her to return to the Underworld.

Persephone set Despoina on her feet beside the antsy foul, she and Arion racing off through the field, Arion charging ahead with Godly speed, while his sister tried to stay upright to follow his lead.

Persephone gave a small shake of her head, giving another smile as she bit her thumb. She was captivating, wearing a gown handmade by her mother. It was the color of wheatgrass, crystals that were sewn into the silky fabric sparkling in her movements when they caught hints of light. Her mother had said she and Hekate had worked on the garment together. It wasn't odd to see Hekate in the mortal world, for she would make occasional visits to them. Persephone had let go of the grudge she held against Hekate, finding that the witch was quite a pleasure to be around. She would keep Persephone company, and help her watch her siblings.

The wind began to pick up, shaking weak tree branches and tearing leaves from them. The grass began to swish, Persephone clinging to the hem of her dress, and squinting her eyes. A rumble of thunder crackled in the sky, the harsh breeze shifting her thick curls over her face. The sun began to vanish behind dreary clouds, darkening their surroundings.

It was then it clicked, Persephone's gaze lighting up as bright as the sun had. She looked to her mother, her jaw slack yet still caught in an excited beam.

Demeter gave her a supportive smile, the snap of reigns and whinnying of horses tore their sights off to the side to witness a chariot. Two shadowy horses harboring black coats hastened the heart of the Goddess. Hekate guided the horses.

"Hades sent me to summon you to the Underworld, my Queen." She winked, Persephone overcome by bliss. Her excitement led her to nearly jump into the chariot without looking back. She managed to gain control over her elation upon remembering Demeter. She faced her disheartened mother, Persephone hitching up her gown, and racing across the field. Drying flower beds crunched under her soles, Persephone reaching her mother, and locking her in a tight embrace. Demeter clutched her daughter's face, placing a heavy kiss on her cheek. Demeter's lips lingered, breathing in the floral scent of her daughter. Finally, Demeter let her go, holding Persephone at arm's length.

"Go now, he's waiting for you."

Persephone dipped her head, rushing back to Hekate with a quick goodbye to her brother and sister. She climbed into the chariot, leaving behind the mortal world for her world with him.

Ruling the undead at his side.

Miles of dying nature passed, withering until her return. A fault opened in the earth, the deep fissure stretching wide enough for the chariot to dart through. The mares leading the chariot charged down the steep walls to the depths below. Endlessly they rode through the blackness, Persephone spotting a faint blue light in the distance. Growing closer, the chariot hit the floor, skidding to a halt. Large gates barely came into view, an even larger guard dog meeting her gaze.

Hekate opened the door, Persephone's cinnamon attention poorly adjusting to the dimly lit tunnel.

Awaiting her hand was Hermes, Persephone beaming in his presence. He returned the gesture, a grin curling his lips.

Persephone soundlessly took his hand, stepping from the chariot. The harsh screeching of opening gates invited Hekate

SEVEN POMEGRANATE SEEDS

inside. She whipped the mares reigns, the crack sending them forth ahead of Persephone and Hermes through the gates. The gust of wind wafted the smell of decay, Persephone remaining unbothered for it was a scent she was accustomed to here. One she hadn't taken in for half a year.

Persephone bowed her head to Cerberus, Cerberus too lowering their three heads to greet her highness.

They neared the Charon boat, the fetor radiating from the black liquid flowing endlessly in the body of splashing decay. Hermes assisted Persephone onto the boat, the boatman silently paddling through the outstretched hands, and woeful cries.

The tunnel came into view, and Persephone's pulse became erratic.

Soon. She would be with him soon.

After assisting her onto land, she linked her arm with Hermes, the Messenger God navigating both she and many souls through the tunnel of the dead. The howls of their misery tingled her spine, the shock spreading from her nape to her fingertips. How eerie yet welcoming their calls were.

A soft glow beckoned her, Hermes taking his time to guide her towards the light that awaited at the end of the tunnel.

Persephone creased her brows, blinded momentarily by the change of lighting as she entered his sanctum. She rapidly blinked, astounded when she opened her eyes. Flowers of deep blues, greens, and blacks welcomed her, the glittering teal lake littered with bloomed magenta lilies, faeries excitedly chirping. They tugged the hem of her dress inside, prying her from Hermes who instead tread behind Persephone.

"Ah, our lovely Queen of the Dead has returned." Neráida's smooth tone cooed, Persephone finding herself gazing at the stunning Queen of Faeries, a leafy emerald dress stopping short of her knees leaving her glowing white skin visible. Her long straight locks stopped just passed her rear, and the twig crown laced with floral pieces still looked adoring on her. If she wasn't mistaken, she would have claimed Neráida to grow more beautiful in her absence. She extended her tender touch of Persephone's cheek, and the young Queen smiled.

Persephone turned to find Medusa, quickly averting her eyes.

"You've grown since I've seen you last, God-*hiss* of Spring." She said, her snake locks curling and winding around one another.

Floating blue, red, and yellow orbs peppered her skin, drawing her forward.

"Queen of the Dead! Queen of the Dead!" The faeries exclaimed in bliss, Persephone smiling as she allowed them to guide her further into his sanctum.

Persephone caught sight of two black-cloaked women, their curves visible as they stood before one another, from their tones, it sounded as if they were bickering.

Iridescent eyes gleamed from beneath her hood, Persephone tearing away from the faeries for a short moment to greet Circe.

It was Hekate who had gazed at Persephone, leading Circe to side eye the Goddess as she neared.

"Persephone, it is nice to see you well." Persephone saw from the sneer in her lip, she was all but elated to see Persephone, nevertheless, Persephone knew that would soon change.

Persephone reached for the thin chain around her neck, ripping away the hidden gift she had saved for months for this moment. Laced through the necklace was a small vial filled with a few drops of Persephone's blood. She held out the jewelry to Circe, who's brows creased in confusion.

Persephone offered a smile taking Circe's hand. She slowly wound the chain into Circe's palm, closing her fingers over it.

"For your troubles, as promised."

"I hadn't committed to keeping you safe-"

"Your loyalty had been enough." Persephone murmured.

The shuffle behind her brought Persephone to gaze over her shoulder, finding a path had been cleared straight to his empty throne.

Persephone lowered her eyes, finding her husband waiting for her, a toothy smile quirking his mouth.

Her heart soared at that moment, blood running hot through her veins. Her wheat colored dress had burst into red flames, Persephone gasping. Hades watched as flakes of ash fell from her gown, the intense red becoming charcoal. Her bloomed skirt became slim, hundreds of obsidian crystals lining the sleek gown. The faeries brought her crown from its stand, placing it on his beloved's head.

Persephone eyed her garment, a beam he had yearned to see for what felt like an eternity was granted to him. He was so desperate for her warmth during her absence, he demanded Hermes describe her smile, and how warm her happiness made the mortal world.

His bride ran to him, tackling him in an eager hug that knocked the wind from his lungs. Her arms laced around his neck, dragging him down to her hungry lips. Fervent, her mouth moved over his, Hades returning the heated desire. His fingers inched along her waist, her touch scaling over his chest.

Now the Underworld could experience the warmth of her light once more.

She cocked her head back from their kiss, his heavy breaths tickling her swollen lips. He rested his forehead to hers, his mouth slanted in a smirk watching the flickering flames in her crossed eyes.

"Welcome home, Persephone."

ABOUT THE AUTHOR

Jasmine Garcia, a part-time author, who works as a full-time nursing assistant. Though time management proves to be a challenge, she is always sure to sneak in a sentence or several here and there. Having been a storyteller long before she was able to put pen to paper, it was no surprise when at seventeen, she became a self-published author. Her works mostly revolve around aspects of romance, magic, paranormal creatures, and lots of gore, so her stories are not for the faint of heart. If such matters interest you, be sure to follow her social medias for more about the author, and to keep up with her new releases!

Printed in Great Britain
by Amazon